CW00521929

# THERE'S A WHIP
# IN MY VALISE

GRETA X

# THERE'S A WHIP
# IN MY VALISE

DELECTUS BOOKS

London

# INTRODUCTION

...And then there was the immensely popular 'Angela Pearson', who occasionally doubled as 'Greta X'. Angela catered to devotees of le vice anglais who were, not surprisingly, mainly English. The titles of her books removed any doubt of their orientation: *The Whipping Club, The Whipping Post, Whips Incorporated* (all from the pen of 'Angela Pearson'), *Whipsdom* and the inspired *There's a Whip in My Valise* (by 'Greta X').

Marilyn Meeske remembered Angela well.

> [She] was at the time *the* popular writer for Olympia. Her speciality was doing the sort of books about governesses who administer punishment. Fan mail...by the carload...Letters began: 'Dear Angela: How did you ever realise my most intimate desire?' Lawyers, physicians, postal inspectors wished to meet her. They were convinced that she was the only one who truly understood them.

But even Angela had to 'crawl through the grey twilight for her pay. Would she be blue-eyed and demure? Would she carry a personalised whip in a special attaché case? Nobody knew because everything had been done through correspondence.'

Finally, the moment of truth.

> A great Englishman entered, with a florid complexion and Coldstream Guard moustache. He was ushered into Girodias's private office. Their conversation was brisk and filled with masculine tones. It was difficult to discern the subject.

However, after a short period of time a rather disturbed but clear British voice boomed, 'Do you think my career would ever be ruined should I be discovered to be Angela Pearson?'

'Angela' did not have to worry because Girodias kept the faith, as he did with all professional confidences between himself and his authors. While not a high priority in my research, I had hoped to take a peek under Angela's veil and had given up when, unexpectedly, I came across an exchange of letters among Girodias's papers.

Olympia's most commercially successful writer was indeed an Englishman who has pursued an eminently respectable career. We entered into a correspondence, and at his request, I have agreed to replace the veil to preserve his anonymity.

The first 'Angela Pearson' book was written, he says, after 'some experiences with two ladies of her persuasion. He sent the manuscript to the Olympia Press and Girodias quickly replied accepting it for publication. Later, author and publisher met in Paris and established a friendly and productive relationship that lasted about seven years. At the first meeting Girodias said that he wanted more 'Angela Pearson' books but later advised a change of name - although not of subject - and came up with 'Greta X'.

The two men lost contact with each other for more than twenty years, when, out of the blue, the author wrote to Girodias expressing his willingness to saddle up and turn out some more Angela Pearson books. Girodias replied explaining the demise of the Olympia Press and the degradation of the genre. But he also came up with an idea. What about 'a spoof on sado-masochism in the form of an amusing pseudo-autobiography, interspersed with excerpts from Angela Pearson books'? This would revive the market for the original books.

'There's a vast fortune to be made with such a book,' he continued, ' but it must be based on some human reality, the author's in the first place, and also the reader's...S & M was very big in the United States when I lived there, and still is, I'm sure; and as to England, wow....'

The author responded modestly by saying the he thought his experiences might be too dull. They mainly featured 'the seduction of a number of likely girls by giving them one or more of the books to read, and then proceeding (or halting) according to their reactions'. But another idea came to mind.

What about something dealing with the Pearson family - in particular Angelica, the daughter of Angela? The daughter *and* the pupil. Like mother, like daughter. Something written autobiographically by Angelica: 'It was on the morning of my seventeenth birthday that my mother opened the door for me to a totally new sexual world.' Something like that. And then on with *her* experiences.

Alas, nothing came of it. Girodias died eighteen months later and Angela packed the whips away in her valise for good.

Extracted from: *The Good Ship Venus: The Erotic Voyage of the Olympia Press* by John De St. Jorre (Pimlico 1995, £10.00)

*Editors note. For Further information on the Olympia Press consult either Mr. De St. Jorre's book mentioned above or the two volume autobiography by Maurice Girodias, the first volume, *The Frog Prince: An Autobiography* (Crown NY 1980), has been translated however the second volume has, so far, only appeared in French. For a full Bibliography consult *The Paris Olympia Press: An Annotated Bibliography* by Patrick Kearney (Black Spring Press London 1987), and his later self-published bibliography of the Olympia Press publications in the U.S.A.

# PART ONE

## 1

Wilhelm Franz-Rüller shook his head apologetically at the three hitch-hikers who waved their hands dejectedly at him, as they stood beside their ruck-sacks on the verge of the road. He felt a little guilty. He was alone in his car, which was a large Rolls-Royce, and there was plenty of room for them, ruck-sacks and all. And they did look quite decent, quite safe. They were probably university students. They were English, too. There was an English flag sewn to one of the ruck-sacks.

He put his foot tentatively to the brake pedal. Perhaps, he thought, he ought to stop for them, after all. Then he remembered some of the chilling stories that appeared constantly in the newspapers about robberies, beatings, even murders, by hitch-hikers who had looked decent and safe to the drivers who picked them up. He moved his foot back to the accelerator.

The Rolls swept up the road with the gentle swish of an approaching gale. In his driving-mirror he watched them sit down on their ruck-sacks.

If they *are* English university students, he thought to himself, it's a great pity. But how can one be certain of hitch-hikers these days? That flag doesn't prove they are English. An English flag — or any other flag, for that matter — can be bought in almost every tourist souvenir-shop all over Europe. And what is to prove they are university students? They may just as easily be thugs.

He recalled, with a shiver, a story he had read only a few weeks ago. A Swiss business-man had picked up two young men on the outskirts of Kiel. They looked like university students. For the first hour or so they were pleasant and stimulating companions, and the Swiss began to congratulate himself for having picked them up. But then one of them drew a gun and ordered him to drive into the first quiet side-road. With a sick feeling of fear he obeyed, and stopped the car immediately he was ordered to do so. As he sat, with pounding heart, wondering what was going to happen next, he was hit hard under his right ear with the butt of the gun.

The two men bundled him, unconscious, out of the driving seat, and one of them took his place. The car was driven into a clearing in some nearby woods. It was parked carefully in a position in which it was screened by bushes and trees from the sight of anyone driving along the road below. The two men dragged the Swiss from the car and emptied his pockets of all his money and valuables. Then they stripped him naked. They picked him up and laid him face downwards over the front of his car. With some cord that they took from their ruck-sacks they tied him securely in this position, with

8

his legs wide open. They found a tin of water in the luggage-boot and poured it over his head to help him to regain consciousness. When he finally came to his senses, they opened the fronts of their trousers and, one after the other, savaged him brutally. Satiated, they sat beside the car, smoking, listening to his moans, and waiting for their virility to return. Then they savaged him again.

Wilhelm Franz-Rüller shivered again. No, he thought. Let other people pick up hitch-hikers, if they want to. A sensible person doesn't take chances.

He looked at the dashboard clock. Six-twenty. With any luck he would be home before midnight.

## 2

Five kilometres further up the road, two beautiful girls sat on a bridge, waiting for a car to pick them up. It was not a busy road and few cars had passed them. The few that had done so, and had failed to stop for them, had all had women sitting beside the drivers. The girls were not at all despondent. They knew they had only to wait for a car that was driven by a man who was alone.

One of them, a blonde, wearing a pair of very well-cut jeans and a light brown suede-leather jacket, was passing her time by firing a small pistol at the various objects that floated on the surface of the slowly-moving stream beneath them.

The other, a red-head, wearing a similar pair of jeans, thrust her hands deep into the pockets of her shiny black kid-leather jacket and said irritably: "I do wish you'd stop playing with that pistol." She spoke in Swedish.

"Why?" said the blonde.

"It gets on my nerves."

"I'm sorry. But it amuses me."

It was the end of a long day, and each was rather irritated with the other.

"Suppose a policeman comes along?" said the red-head.

"All right. So?"

"Do you think he'd like you taking pot-shots at the river?"

"Why not? We have a permit."

"We have a permit to carry a pistol for self-defence, not for taking a pot-shot at anything that catches our fancy."

The blonde sighed and put the pistol in her pocket. "All right. But you're in an awfully bad mood."

"So are you."

The blonde smiled suddenly, a warm humorous expression lighting up her face. "Yes. I suppose I am. I'm sorry."

The other responded at once to her smile. "I'm sorry, too. It's been a long day."

The blonde put her chin on her hands. "I know what would make me feel better."

"What?"

"A man."

The red-head laughed. "You're really awful, you know. How anyone can be such a nymphomaniac beats me."

The blonde raised her eyebrows. "Look who's talking!"

"I'm not a nymphomaniac."

"Perhaps not. But you have other perversions."

"Yes, perhaps I have. But they're under control."

"More or less."

"More than yours, anyway."

"I'm not ashamed of being a nymph. I wish some

man would come along now." She took the pistol out of her pocket. "I'd make him do just what I want. He'd take off his trousers and—"

"Sshhh! I think I hear a car."

They stood up and looked along the road. A Rolls-Royce came into view. It was moving fast. They stepped into the middle of the road, waving their arms. As far as they could see, the driver seemed to be a man, and he seemed to be alone.

### 3

Wilhelm Franz-Rüller saw the two girls standing in the middle of the road, waving their arms at him. Automatically he put his hand to the horn. They jumped quickly back to the verge as he swept by them.

He put his foot quickly on the brake. He had seen that they were very beautiful. He had also seen that they were both wearing leather jackets, and he had a strong perverted fetish for leather jackets that were worn by beautiful women. With no memory of his decision of a few minutes ago not to take chances with hitch-hikers, he put the car into reverse and backed towards the bridge.

The girls picked up their ruck-sacks and opened the doors of the Rolls. The red-head got into the front, the blonde into the back. They disposed their ruck-sacks on the other end of the back seat.

"Thank you very much," said the red-head in German. "You are German, aren't you? You have a German number."

"Yes," said Wilhelm Franz-Rüller, his eyes on their leather jackets, "I am German. But you are not, huh?"

"No, we are Swedes. And we don't speak German very well."

"You speak it beautifully."

"Thank you, but that is not true."

"Where are you heading for?"

"Kiel."

He made sure that their doors were shut, and drove off again. "How nice for me. I am going to Kiel, too."

They drove for some time in silence. Then: "Are you going to Kiel for a holiday?" he asked.

"A sort of holiday," answered the blonde, from the back of the car. "A friend of ours is a governess there."

"A governess? With which family? Perhaps I know them."

"A Swede called Per Petersen. Do you live in Kiel?"

"Yes. And I know Per Petersen. His wife died six months ago."

"That was when our friend became the governess of his children."

"I see. Yes, I remember something about that. How curious our meeting like this."

"Yes, isn't it?" said the blonde. "Will you forgive me if I speak to my friend in Swedish? I find it rather a strain to go on in German."

"Of course. Please do so."

"Do you speak Swedish yourself?"

"Unfortunately not."

The blonde crossed her legs. "Fortunately," she said in Swedish, "not unfortunately. What do you think of him?"

"Very nice," said the red-head. "Young, tall, handsome. Yes, nice."

"*Very* nice indeed," said the blonde, drawing her breath through her lips. "I want him."

The red-head turned quickly in her seat. "No! For God's sake, get a hold on yourself. Don't be stupid. This is our ride to Kiel, without any further trouble."

"I want him," repeated the blonde stubbornly. She drew the pistol out of her pocket and covered it on her lap with her hands.

"Are you completely off your head?" said the red-head angrily. "Put that thing away. Do try to control your damn nymphomania!"

"I want him," said the other again. She spoke in a voice that was almost without expression. "And you can do to him the things that you like doing."

"I don't want to do anything to him at all."

"Don't you? What about that lovely whip in your bag that's crying out to be used? And what about the dildo?"

"You really are absolutely mad! Don't you remember? You told him where we're going. You told him we're going to Per Petersen's house to see Margarete."

"So what? Don't you want to use your lovely whip?"

"Oh, for Christ's sake! I couldn't now, even if I did want to. He knows who we are."

"No, he doesn't. He doesn't know anything about us, except that we're friends of Margarete. And that doesn't prevent us having him, does it?"

Wilhelm Franz-Rüller cleared his throat. "You seem to be quarrelling." He took out his cigarette case. "Do you smoke?"

The red-head took two and handed one to the blonde. "Thank you. No, we're not quarrelling. We're just having a difference of opinion."

He produced his lighter. His eyes were on her jacket as he lit her cigarette. She passed it to the blonde and took back the unlighted cigarette. She bent her head again to light the second cigarette.

"That's a very beautiful coat," he said.

13

"Thank you," she said, and smiled suddenly. "But I wonder why you say so. There's nothing very special about it. It's just a leather jacket."

"It's a very beautiful one," he said. He wished he could run his hand over its surface.

She stared quizzically at him. Then, slowly and deliberately, she put her hands flat upon the surface of the jacket above her breasts. She let them remain there for a moment and then she drew them downwards towards her stomach. "If you don't look where you're going," she said, "we're going to have a nasty accident." His eyes had been fixed upon her for some seconds.

He jerked his head back to the road.

"Fortunately," she said, "it's a fairly empty road. But you must keep your on eyes on it — and not on my jacket." She paused for a moment. "Have you a fetish for leather?"

He seemed to swallow. "A fetish for leather? No, of course not. What do you mean?"

She chuckled, and turned her head to the blonde. "All right," she said, in Swedish. "I'm with you, you nymph! Let's have him, and to hell with everything else."

"I was hoping you'd see reason," said the blonde coolly. "But I don't understand why you change your mind just because he's got a fetish for leather."

"Nor do I. But I'm all for it now."

The blonde uncovered the pistol that had been hidden in her hands. "And what about all your objections because he knows who we are?"

"As *you* said, he *doesn't* know who we are."

"Exactly. And Margarete can't be made to suffer for what her friends may or may not do."

"No, of course she can't." The red-head seemed to tremble suddenly. "How are we going to do it?"

The blonde said: "You just leave it to me." She

raised the pistol in her right hand and put its muzzle lightly to the ear of the driver. "Do you feel this?" she asked, in German. "Don't turn round."

He turned round immediately, as he felt the cold steel against his ear.

"I said that you must not turn round," said the blonde. "Look in front of you. Do you want us to have an accident?"

"What do you want?" he said, his voice showing the fear that had struck to his bowels at the sight of the gun.

"Just do as you're told, and everything will be all right."

"But, damn it all!" he began to bluster. "You can't get away with—"

She pressed the pistol harder against his ear. "Just do as you're told."

There was a silence for a few moments. Then: "If you want money," he said, "I'll give you what I have. I'll give it quite willingly. But do please put that pistol away. It makes me nervous."

The red-head laughed. "That's very nice of you. But we don't want any of your money."

"The car, then?"

"Neither the car. What should we do with a car like this?"

"What *do* you want then?"

She cupped her hands to her leather-covered breasts again. "You'll find out soon enough."

"Now, in fact," said the blonde suddenly. "Turn off the road there at that lane on the left."

"Oh Christ!" murmured the man, and put his foot to the brake. He was remembering again the story of the Swiss business-man. But these were girls, he told himself. There must be some other reason for their wanting to turn into a side lane.

15

He swung the car into the lane, and proceeded slowly.

The blonde looked about her. "Yes," she said. "You see those woods up there on the left. Drive up there."

He began to feel sick with fear. "Why? Why do you want to go up there? What are you going to do?"

She chuckled. "What I'm going to do to you myself may be rather pleasant for you. You'll probably like it very much. What my friend is going to do to you is quite a different matter."

"What are you going to do?"

"I?" She drew on her cigarette. "I'm going to let you make love to me."

He turned his head again. "You can't be serious."

"Look in front of you. Yes, I'm quite serious."

"But you don't have to pull a gun on me to make me do that. It's a wonderful idea."

"Good. I'm glad you think so. But the gun makes sure of everything. I didn't want any argument. And a man sometimes does argue very stupidly when a girl makes a pass at him. He likes to be the big he-man and make the pass himself."

The red-head interrupted. "My friend, you see, is a nymphomaniac. Anything in trousers will do very well for her. The fact that you're presentable makes things a good deal better — but I don't think it would have made any difference if you'd been a dwarf."

"I see." He was silent for a moment. "She said you're going to do something different."

"Yes."

"What are you going to do?"

"Whip you," said the red-head simply.

"What?"

"I'm going to whip you."

"Why?"

"I'm a sadist."

"Good God!" The fear, which had begun to recede, now flooded back. "Good God! I've heard of women like you."

They had reached the edge of the woods.

"Drive off the road," ordered the blonde, "and find some secluded spot."

"But," he protested, "look at that ground. It'll ruin the car. It'll break a spring or something."

"Not if you drive carefully. Go on. Do as I say. I don't want a car like this standing at the side of the road and bringing the whole countryside snooping around."

He looked for the most even surface, and slowly drove the car off the road. It bumped up a small incline and was soon inside the woods.

"Stop here," said the blonde. "This'll do very well." She held out her hand. "Give me the car-key."

He took the key from the dashboard and handed it to her silently.

"Thank you," she said, and opened her door. "Come on. Get out, and meet your fate." She looked at the red-head. "Why don't you tell him what else you're going to do to him?" She continued to speak in German.

The red-head shook her head. "Let him find out, after his whipping. Do you want him first?"

"Yes, please. But there's no reason why you shouldn't stimulate him a bit while he's doing it."

"No, there isn't. I'll give him quite a stimulation, too." The red-head was out of the car too, and was fumbling with the zip of her ruck-sack.

The man watched her with narrowed eyes. He thought he knew what she was looking for, and tried to persuade himself that he was wrong. When she

17

drew a long coiled whip and several lengths of rope out of the ruck-sack he felt sick and cold. "For Christ's sake," he said, "you're not going to use *that*, are you?"

The red-head uncoiled the whip. It was about a metre in length. "Yes," she said silkily. "What else?"

"Get your clothes off," said the blonde.

"Now, look!" he protested. "This is all going too far. I'd love to make love to you, both of you — but please put that whip away. I'm sure you're not serious."

"No?" said the red-head softly. She raised the whip and brought it down hard across the front of his legs. He yelled with pain. "What would you say now?" she asked. "Am I serious or not?"

"Yes," he gasped. "But please don't be."

"That's better. Now get undressed. Quickly."

"We'll have to gag him," said the blonde. "That noise could be heard a long way away. What'll happen when you really start?"

"Yes," said the red-head. "We'll gag him." She put her hand back into her ruck-sack and took out a pair of silk stockings. "These will do very well."

He stood there watching her, wondering what to do. He could quite easily overpower them if he chose his moment carefully. He turned his head to the blonde. The pistol was still in her hand.

"I think I know what you're thinking," she said. "But I'll shoot you if you make any trouble. Not to kill, of course. But I'll shoot you in the leg or the foot. And I'm quite a good shot. Look down at that leaf beside your left foot."

He looked down at the leaf.

She pulled the trigger.

He jumped at the unexpected noise. A small round hole appeared in the centre of the leaf.

"Do you see what I mean?" she said.

The red-head said angrily: "Are you crazy? Do you want to bring the whole neighbourhood? For God's sake don't use that thing just for the fun of it."

"You're right," said the blonde. "Sorry. The sooner we get him tied up the better."

"Will you please—?" he began.

"No," said the red-head. "We won't, whatever it is. Now get undressed, damn you." She swung her whip again. It cracked across his shoulders. He gave another yell. "Quickly! Come on, strip!"

He drew a quick breath and began to take off his clothes. When he was naked, the red-head put down the whip and took a length of rope in her hands. She went behind him. "Put your hands behind your back." She tied his wrists expertly. "That's better." She looked at the blonde. "Now you can put that damn gun away."

"All right," said the other, and put the pistol into her pocket. She undid the zip of her jeans and pushed them down to her ankles. Stepping out of them, she said: "This ground is a bit rough. We'd better have a blanket or something." She turned to the naked man. "Have you got one in the car?"

"Yes," he said, his eyes on her shapely legs. "In the luggage compartment."

"Where's the key?"

"It's open."

She went to the back of the car and fetched a rich-looking plaid rug. "You must be quite well-off," she said, as she spread it on the ground. "Everything you have is very expensive. Who are you?"

The red-head stooped and took his wallet out of the jacket he had thrown to the ground. She opened it and took out a card. "He is the Baron Wilhelm Franz-Rüller of Koburg-See. Hmmm. Is he, indeed?

19

It's the first time I've whipped a baron." She put the wallet back into his pocket. She picked up the whip.

The blonde lay down on the rug and wriggled out of her pants. She held up her arms. "All right, my baron. You can come and excite me now."

"Wait a minute," said the red-head. "I must gag him first."

"Not yet, for God's sake. I need his mouth too."

"Yes, of course. But he's going to make a lot of noise."

"Don't whip him too hard, then. Just stimulate him a bit. In any case I don't want you whipping him into impotency. Wait till I've finished. You can gag him afterwards when you start on him yourself."

"All right," said the red-head. She swished the whip through the air. It made a fearful seething noise. "But don't take too long."

The man gazed at her in awe. He had till that moment been half-hoping that she was not serious about whipping him, that she had only been trying, for some reason or other, to frighten him. Now he saw the look in her eyes as she swished her dreadful whip. It had a terrifying light of calculated cruelty. He watched her draw the whip slowly, almost caressingly, through the fingers of her free hand. His faint hope died away. He shivered.

He looked wildly around the clearing, pulling at the ropes that bound his wrists. They did not give as much as a millimetre. He wondered whether he should run for it. He was so frightened that his nakedness did not matter in the least. But he doubted whether, with his hands tied behind him, he could run faster than the girls. He would probably lose his balance and trip. And then what would this terrible girl do to him with her whip? Anger would be added to calculated cruelty. And yet... if he could reach the road... and start shouting... Somebody might — just might — be within earshot. But then, what about the gun? Would the blonde dare to do as she had threatened? She had proved she was a good enough shot, but surely she wouldn't dare...

The red-head seemed to read his thoughts. She picked up another length of rope. "It would be most unwise to try to run away. But you're probably frightened enough to try it. So I'll just tie your ankles and make sure of you. I don't want that damn gun being used." She moved beside him, looped the whip round his neck, and stooped to his feet. She quickly tied his ankles tightly together. "Now you'll have to jump when you want to move." She stood up and took the whip back into her hand.

"Come on, come on!" said the blonde, from the rug. "What are you waiting for?"

He turned his head and looked down at her. She had let her arms fall to her sides. She had opened the front of her suede-leather jacket and her silk blouse. Except for a tiny brassiere she was naked underneath them. She was very lovely. He caught his breath sharply and felt desire flood through him. Momentarily he forgot his fear of the other girl and her whip. He gazed at the blonde hair of the mound, and at the long shapely legs stretched lazily out on the rug. And he gazed at the soft suede-leather jacket and wished his hands were free to touch it. His penis began to grow.

He made a number of small hops until he reached the side of the rug. He bent his legs and knelt. "It's damned difficult with my hands and legs tied like this."

"Never mind. Come on. Put your mouth to my

breasts." She put a hand to the brassiere and pulled the breasts free. They were large and firm.

Still kneeling, he bent his body downwards and put his lips first to one and then to the other.

She put up a hand and took hold of his penis. Due to his condition of fear it had been only half-erected. Now, at her touch, it grew to its full erected size. She caressed it lightly and then let her fingers play delicately with the bag of his testicles. She began to breathe in quick gasps.

The red-head also began to breathe quickly as she looked at the man's kneeling posture, his head down to the blonde's breasts and his bottom high up and tightly stretched. She drew her whip through her fingers again and moved into position a few feet away from him, on his left. She raised the whip slowly to the height of her shoulder, poised it there for a second as she took careful aim with her eye, and then brought it down quite lightly across the exact centre of his buttocks.

In spite of the relative lightness of the lash, he jerked upright as though he had received an electric shock. He had been more surprised than hurt, for he had temporarily forgotten about the whip. "No!" he exclaimed. "No, no!"

"Yes!" said the red-head, and struck him again in the same place. "But what are you complaining about? These are loving caresses."

"Damn you!" said the blonde. "Get your head down here again. Don't stop like that. I'll thrash you myself if you stop again. Get down here. Lie down over me." She pulled hard on his penis.

He rolled heavily over on to his side and straightened himself over her body. He wriggled himself downwards until his lips came again to her breasts. He opened his mouth and sucked a nipple on to his tongue.

22

The red-head changed her position and struck again with her whip. He gave a flinch but did not move his lips. He instinctively thrust his bound hands downwards as though to protect his buttocks. The next lash caught him across his knuckles. He quickly took his hands out of danger; the pain to them was worse than the pain to the muscles of his bottom.

The blonde was gasping again. She put her hands to his head and pushed. "Go down to my fanny. Lick my fanny."

He obeyed at once, receiving two more lashes before he was in position. He put his face to the silky blonde hairs of her mound. She opened her legs, lifted them over his shoulders, and then closed them tightly against his head. She took hold of his hair with both hands and pulled it, forcing his face closer to her vagina. She began to utter long moans of pleasure.

With his tongue he felt for the lips of her vagina. He licked them up and down lightly at first and then, as his passion mounted, roughly. He twisted his jaw against the pressure of her legs and took the lips in his teeth. She gave a little cry. He moved his head down a little, buried his nose between the lips and thrust his tongue into her passage.

The whip continued to lash across his buttocks. He found that the pain was not by any means unendurable. He would not have said it was pleasant, but it gave a stimulation to his passion. He wished his arms and legs were free. He would not now have run away. He would have used them to improve the efficiency of his love-making. It was a pity, for instance, that his fingers could not be playing with her nipples.

The red-head went on swinging her whip quite lightly, but she felt no interest, no excitement. She wanted to hit with all her strength. Then she would feel the savage uplift of delectability, the straining rapture of pure pleasure. She wished the blonde would hurry up. She tried not to look at the naked back of the man, with its weal across the shoulders from the hard lash she had given him before he undressed. She knew that she would not be able to control herself if she looked at it. Its expanse of unwhipped flesh would magnetise her too much. She would be forced to give at least one hard lash across its centre, and that would assuredly reduce his erection to immediate limpness. And that would mean that the blonde would take even longer to finish.

The man was beginning to feel a good deal of discomfort from a lack of sufficient air. The blonde's legs gripped his head ever more tightly as her excitement mounted. He tried to lift his head for a second, but found it firmly locked into its position.

The blonde looked up at her friend. "I've forgotten a french-letter. Be a dear and get one for me, will you? I don't want a baby."

"Are you ready to have him?"

"Almost."

The red-head went to her ruck-sack and took out a small packet. She came back to the rug and tore off the silver paper. She put the rubber to her lips and blew gently. The teat filled up at once with air. "Yes," she said. "It's all right."

The blonde opened her legs. She sighed deeply. "That was very nice. Now turn over on your side for a moment."

He did as she said.

The red-head looped the whip round his neck again and knelt to put the letter on his now gigantic penis. She gave it a small slap with her palm.

"Wet it a little, please," said the blonde.

The red-head worked her tongue to gather some saliva, and then spat into her palm. She rubbed the moisture over the tip of the rubber. "Right," she said. "You're ready." She took the whip back into her hand.

"Hutch up, then," the blonde said to the man. "And make it very sweet for me or I'll make it very painful for you afterwards."

"Can't you untie me?" he said.

"No. I like the idea of your being like that. Come on, hutch yourself up." She opened her legs.

With some difficulty he moved himself jerkily into position over her. She took his penis in her hands and guided it to her vagina. His penis grew even larger under her touch. He felt it nose against the mouth of her passage. He pushed. She was tight. He pushed again.

The red-head raised her whip. "I'll help you," she said softly. She lashed again across the buttocks, but this time the lash was considerably harder.

He flinched violently with the pain, and cried out for the first time. His flinch drove his penis deep inside the blonde. She flung her arms around his neck and sank her nails into the flesh of his shoulder-blades. She gave a cry of pleasure.

He withdrew a little, preparing to make another natural thrust with his hip muscles. He buried his head into the leather of her jacket.

The red-head struck again, as hard as before.

His flinch made the thrust for him. He felt he had never before been so far inside a woman. He realized that his penis was fully engulfed.

Another hard lash showed him he was wrong. It went even further inside the passage. He left it where it was, waiting for the next lash. He felt it could not possibly go any deeper.

The lash showed him that he was wrong again.

He began to realise why so many men willingly submitted to a thrashing while making love. Without the stimulus of a whip nobody could ever penetrate so deeply as he had now done. He found, too — much to his surprise — that the pain was becoming less unbearable with each lash. His bottom felt as though it was on fire, and white-hot needles seemed to be stabbing at its nerves — but there was at the same time a suggestion of pleasure beneath the pain, some hitherto untasted pleasure which he realised was quite extra, which had no direct relation to the ordinary joy of love-making, and which was caused by the now-agonising, now-stimulating, lashes of the whip. He began to withdraw and thrust with his hip muscles now, but he timed his thrusts with the hiss of the whip as it descended. He felt his gathering ejaculation sending its waves of ecstasy through his loins, and fought to control it. He did not dare to think of what would happen if he finished before the blonde.

She lay tense, in another world. His penis, with its violent thrusts, seemed to reach up as far as her stomach. Her body quivered from head to toe as she answered his thrusts. Once, the tip of the whip curled too far round his bottom and cut into the side of her leg. She hardly noticed the pain. She was as though anaesthetised by sheer bliss.

Suddenly her body stiffened. She sank her nails deeply into his back as the poignant ecstasy possessed her.

He at once abandoned his control of himself, and allowed his violence a free rein.

The red-head gave a sigh, the sigh of one who has waited too patiently and too long for something badly needed. She shifted her position a little and aimed her whip at his back. With all her force she brought it down across the shoulder-blades. It was quite safe now. No pain could interrupt an ejaculation once it had begun.

He gave a sort of shuddering groan as the new agony struck him, but otherwise he took no notice. He sank himself into the savagery of his fulfilment, marvelling, with some small conscious corner of his brain, that such wondrous sensations could exist.

The sensations lasted for quite a long time, and the red-head was able to deliver several more lashes before the spasmodic convulsions of the two bodies began to lessen in force. Only then did she let her whip fall to her side. She paused for a moment and then threw it lightly down beside them.

She wetted her lips. Her own time had come, and she was very ready for it. The last few hard lashes had considerably increased her appetite for what she was going to do. She went to her ruck-sack again and took out another length of rope. She put it on the ground and rummaged about at the bottom of the ruck-sack. She took out a package that was wrapped in plastic. She removed the plastic and looked hungrily at the object it had been protecting.

It was a large double dildo made of a V of hard rubber. The part of the V that would slide inside her own vagina was ten centimetres long; the other part, the part that would stand up in front of her like an enormous erected penis, was fifteen centimetres long. To its base was attached a thick, flat piece of rubber that would lie upon her mound when the dildo was secured into its position by the various straps that now dangled from it.

She balanced the apparatus upon the coil of rope, making sure that the part which would go inside her own passage did not touch the ground. She unzipped her jeans and slipped them down to her ankles. She pushed her panties down after them, and stepped out of both at the same time. She picked up the dildo, parted her legs, and put the shorter end to her vagina. Slowly she pushed it into herself, feeling a sweet rapture as it made its way fully home. She fastened the straps into position round her legs, thighs and waist. She put her hand to the enormous hard rubber penis that now stood away from her stomach at a slight angle. She agitated it, feeling the answering genital sensation as the agitation communicated itself to the end of the V which lay snugly inside her. She began to breathe fast.

She was not a lesbian. She had never yet used the dildo on a woman. Her use of it would probably have given a good deal of surprise to its manufacturer. She used it on the men she whipped. Her supreme sexual gratification came from tying a man into a totally helpless position — face down and with his legs wide open — giving him a merciless thrashing, and then savaging his bottom with her dildo. This action gave her mental as well as physical pleasure. The mental joy was that of subjugating a member of the so-called superior sex with a flogging and a rape; the physical pleasure came from the agitation of the part of the dildo that was inside her as she thrust the other part into her victim. The victim had to be a male man, however; she had no interest in pansies.

She looked now at the two bodies lying on the rug. They were so still that they might have been asleep. The man's back had livid weals across it, and two had begun to bleed a little. His bottom, which she had not hit hard, was criss-crossed by lighter weals and was a flaming red in colour.

She went up to them and picked up her whip. As she walked her great dildo swayed from side to side. "Come on," she said, giving the man a light kick in his ribs. "You've relaxed enough. Get up."

He turned his head and looked up at her. He gave a gasp. From his prostrate position the dildo seemed even larger than it really was. He gazed at it for several moments in shocked fascination, seeing at the same time that her legs were bare and her shiny black leather jacket was still being worn. He took his eyes away from the dildo and looked more closely at her legs. They were extremely shapely. He looked up at her leather jacket and caught his breath. The suede into which he had just been burying his face had excited him greatly, but he had a stronger fetish for soft shiny kid. He felt the faint stirrings of sex, and reflected that they must be in his mind; his body had been drained only a few minutes ago.

He looked back at the dildo and thought that perhaps he was not going to be whipped at once. The red-head must be a lesbian, and must now be waiting for him to get out of her way so that she could herself make love to her friend. If only he could wriggle his wrists out of their ropes while she was doing it... He could then quickly untie his feet and make a get-away. He might even be able to get away in his car. Then he remembered that the blonde had the engine key in her pocket. Never mind. He would grab some of his clothes and run. He could worry about the car later.

He raised his hips and pulled his now flaccid penis out of the blonde's vagina. She lay still with her eyes closed and made no sound. He rolled over on to his side.

"Would you help me up?" he said. "It's a bit difficult, tied up like this."

"With pleasure," said the red-head. "Anything to speed matters up." She put a hand under one of his arms and helped him to stand. "Now," she said, "hop over to the back of your car." She pulled away the wet french-letter.

"Why?"

"Don't ask questions. Do as I say."

He glanced at the whip in her hand and decided to obey her without further words. He hopped, twenty centimetres at a time, to the back of the Rolls. He saw her pick up another coil of rope.

So she's going to tie me up, he said to himself. That's a pity. But if she takes her time with the blonde I might still manage to untie myself.

"Face the car," she ordered. "And lie forward over the back of it."

The metal felt cold against his skin as he lay down over the curved luggage-boot. He wondered why she had to put him into this position. If it was simply to immobilise him, it seemed unnecessarily complicated. Unless — a wave of cold fear ran through him — she intended to thrash him before she made love to her friend. This would probably be a good position for him to be in, if she was going to do that.

He moistened his lips. "Why are you putting me over the back like this?"

"You'll see very soon."

He felt her untying the rope around his ankles. "Are you going to use that whip?"

She laughed. "What a silly question! Of course I am. I told you I was going to, didn't I?"

He made no reply. Hope died again inside him, and at the same time the burning pain in his back seemed to increase. He had been able to ignore it while there was a hope that he could escape. Now it began to claw at him. His heart thumped with terror.

He remembered the Swiss business-man again. He had been tied over his car, too. But it had been for a different purpose: a rape of the bottom, not a whipping. Perhaps the Swiss had been luckier. This fiendish girl would excite herself with her whip, would probably nearly kill him, and would then leave him in his agony while she flung herself and her monstrous dildo upon the body of her friend.

"Open your legs," she said. "Wide."

He opened his legs as widely as he could.

"Wider," she said.

"I can't." Why, for heaven's sake, did she want his legs open?

"You're asking for it, aren't you?" she said. "Do as I say, or you'll repent it so much."

He forced his legs open a few centimetres more.

She knelt beside his left leg and tied a length of rope around the ankle. She threw its free end under the car, beside the left wheel. She stood up and moved forward to the wheel. She knelt again and reached under the car to take the end of the rope. She pulled it tight, passed it round the front and side of the wheel, and knotted it firmly to the part that disappeared under the car. She went round to his right leg and did the same thing with another length of rope. She stood back and regarded her work. "Yes," she said. "You're safe enough like that."

Safe enough, he thought. She said safe enough. So perhaps all this *is* only to stop me running away. But why, why should she want my legs open like this?

"Now your arms," she said, and untied the ropes around his wrists. "I wonder whether there's enough rope." She gathered the remaining pieces and knotted them into one length. "Yes, perhaps." She tied one end round his right wrist. "Stretch your arm upwards, as far as you can." She went to the right-hand rear door of the car, opened it, and let down the window. She shut the door again, tossed the end of the rope through the window on to the seat, walked round the car, opened the left-hand door and let down the window, shut the door again, and reached through the open window for the end of the rope. She pulled tightly on it.

"Ouch!" he exclaimed, as his arm was stretched towards the window of the car. "You'll pull my arm out of its socket!"

"That would be nice," she said, and came back to his side, holding the rope taut. "Put this arm up now."

He stretched his left arm up in front of him.

She wound the end of the rope tightly round his wrist and made some expert knots.

"You *have* got him nice and helpless," said the voice of the blonde.

He turned his head sharply. She was standing beside the car, watching the actions of the red-head with a light of amusement in her eyes.

"Please," he said. "Please go and lie down again."

She raised her eyebrows in surprise. "Lie down again? Why should I?"

"So that" — he hesitated, wondering whether he was being unwise to say it — "so that you'll be ready for her the moment she wants you."

"The moment *who* wants me?"

"Your friend."

"What are you talking about? Why should she want me? What for?"

"To make love to you. If you're not ready on the rug, she'll probably go on longer with that whip."

The blonde looked at the red-head, looked down at the dildo, and burst into laughter. "Oh, the innocent! He thinks you're going to use that on *me!*"

For a second he was puzzled. Then the truth

dawned on him. So that was why she had opened his legs. So the Swiss had not, after all, been luckier. It was going to be both rape and a whipping.

"No," he said, weakly. "No, please. You're not going to put that into me, are you?"

"Yes," said the red-head. "Right into you. As far as it will go."

"No, *please* no!"

"But I'm going to warm you up first, of course. And I'm quite ready to start. Where are those stockings?"

"Here," said the blonde, and gave them to her.

"Please no," he repeated, desperately. "What have I ever done to you?"

The blonde laughed. "Nothing, my dear. But you don't have to have done anything, if you fall into the clutches of a nymph and a sadist. It's just your bad luck, that's all. But don't worry. She won't kill you."

The red-head took hold of a handful of his hair. "Open your mouth."

He gave up struggling against his fate, and opened his mouth. She thrust one rolled-up stocking into it, and tied it into place with the other.

The blonde took the whip into her hand. "Let me give him the first few, please."

"You're a greedy hog," said the red-head. "You've had your pleasure."

"Just a few little lashes. Please."

"All right. But be quick. I don't know why you want to, anyway. You're not a sadist."

"I'm beginning to be. It comes from watching you. And you told me yourself that every woman is a sadist at heart."

"Yes. All right, go ahead. But please be quick."

The blonde put herself into position and swung the whip. She aimed at the fleshy part of his legs,

33

ten centimetres below his bottom. The stroke was very hard. A livid weal sprang to life, and with it some drops of blood.

A terrible, searing pain racked him. A choked moan escaped through the stocking in his mouth.

She swung the whip again, aiming this time at his shoulders. She put all her force into the lash. She felt a quivering pleasure in her loins at the thought of the pain she was giving. Her third lash cut across his buttocks. Her fourth and fifth across the centre of his back.

Panting with excitement more than with exertion, she handed the whip to the red-head. "Thank you. That was very nice indeed." She picked up her pants and jeans and put them on. "And now I'll watch you getting your own pleasure. It always gives me nearly as much of a thrill as anything else." She sat down on the ground and lay back on an elbow.

The red-head drew the now blood-wet whip through her fingers again, and looked hungrily at the naked body that squirmed and strained against its bonds.

She took up her position and drew a deep breath. She began to lash him across the upper part of his back. The lashes followed one another fast. The noise of *swish-crack, swish-crack, swish-crack* cut through the stillness of the woods.

He felt his brain reeling with the intolerable agony. He felt he would go mad with it... if his heart did not burst first. He tried to shriek through his gag, but could find neither the strength nor the breath.

The red-head's heart was also pounding madly. She delivered another dozen lashes and then threw down the whip. She threw herself over his bleeding back and legs, took the end of her dildo in her hands and put its tip to his anus. She gave a great thrust.

34

The dildo slid smoothly into the anal passage. She gave another thrust. The whole length of the dildo disappeared. She began to withdraw and thrust, savouring the blissful sensation inside her vaginal passage as the long end of the dildo communicated its pressures to the short end.

He hardly realised, at first, what was happening to him. The pain that burned his back was so intense that he did not notice the new burn inside his bottom. He knew only that the whipping had stopped. Gradually he became aware, however, of a thrusting and withdrawing movement in his bottom, and he realised that he was being savaged. His first reaction was one of revulsion, but this was followed quickly by the recognition that it was far better to be savaged than whipped. He hoped, dully, that she would quickly satisfy herself, and let him go.

She felt the juices of her culmination gathering. She reduced the speed of her thrusting and withdrawing, letting the impending culmination recede a little, titillating it, tantalising it. Soon it became demanding once more, and began to rise inexorably to its peak. She pulled herself abruptly away from him, and stood panting for a moment. The culmination receded again.

She picked up the whip.

Her lashes were given less rapidly this time. After each *swish-crack* she would pause for a moment, letting the rapture of flagellation do the titillating of the culmination. A wave of hot ecstasy seemed to pour itself over all her genital nerves each time the whip struck.

The blonde began to frown. "Do be careful," she murmured. "You'll kill him if you don't stop soon."

The red-head heard her words but did not at first appreciate their meaning. Then she turned her head. "Perhaps you're right." She spoke in a voice that did not seem her own. But I don't want to finish yet."

"I think you'd better."

"All right. Just six more. I'll let myself come while I give them."

"I hope he doesn't· have a heart attack or something. He's in a terrible state."

"He'll be all right. It takes more than this to kill a man of his size." She contracted her stomach muscles, and felt the culmination give a leap forward as the dildo moved inside her. She raised the whip again. As it struck·she did not try to control the further leap of the culmination. She struck again. "I'm coming now," she murmured. "Oh, oh, oh!" She struck again, and again...

Her culmination rose to its peak and took her in its possession. It shook her and made her tremble from head to toe. And still she lashed with her whip, not knowing that she was doing so, knowing only that she was in another world, a world of unbelievable delight.

The blonde rose quickly to her feet and went to her side. She seized the whip in her hand. "Stop it, for God's sake! That's enough."

"Ooooh!" The red-head gave a moan of shuddering satisfaction and dropped, like a sack, to the ground. She lay there, her eyes closed, breathing very fast.

The blonde looked anxiously at the back of the victim. It was covered with deep weals and running blood. She moved forward and took a handful of his hair. She raised his head gently and looked at his face. His eyes were shut. She put a hand beneath him and felt his heart. To her intense relief it was beating, though far too fast. She began to untie the ropes of his ankles, wondering what

36

they were going to do with him now. They couldn't just leave him in the woods in this condition.

By the time she had untied all the ropes, the red-head opened her eyes, shook her head gently, and smiled. "My, my! That was very nice."

"You went too far," said the other, crossly. "Look at him. Whatever are we going to do with him now?"

"What do you mean? What *should* we do with him?"

"We can't leave him here."

"Whyever not? It's what we always do."

"You don't usually go as far as this. Look at him."

"All right. I'm looking at him. What about it?"

"He needs a doctor, or a hospital."

The red-head sighed. "Oh, do stop being stupid. Are you suggesting that we should drive him to a hospital?"

"No. But we can't leave him here like this."

"What do you suggest then?"

"I don't know," said the blonde stubbornly. "But we can't leave him. It might be ages before anyone found him here, and he's in no condition to do any walking."

"All right, then," said the red-head, getting to her feet and unstrapping the dildo. "We'll put him on the back seat and drive him down to the main road. We'll leave him there. He'll be found in no time. But we'll have to look slippy ourselves, or else we'll be found in no time too. That's why I don't like it." She put the dildo back into its plastic, and picked up her jeans and pants. "Does that satisfy you?"

"Yes. It's the least we can do." The blonde went to where the rug was, picked it up and brought it back to the car. She opened one of the rear doors and spread the rug over the seat. "That'll protect his leather."

The red-head watched her with narrowed eyes. "Have you gone soft on him or something?"

"Don't be silly," said the other shortly. "It's a pity to spoil a car like this, that's all. Come on. Help me lift him." She moved to the back of the car and put a hand under one of his arms. "It's all over," she said. "Can you stand up?"

He made no reply.

"You've forgotten to take out his gag," said the red-head.

"So I have." The blonde untied the stocking at the back of his head and removed his gag. "Can you stand up?" she repeated.

There was still no reply.

"Come on," she said to the red-head. "Help me."

Together, they led him stumblingly to the back seat and helped him to lie down. He made a number of moans, gave a great sigh, and lay still. The blonde covered him with the free end of the rug.

"Time to go," she said. "Do you want to drive, or shall I?"

"You. I'm too exhausted."

"Good. I've always wanted to drive a Rolls-Royce."

They gathered their various belongings and packed them into their ruck-sacks. They climbed into the car, looked once at the silent man, and shut the doors. The blonde took the engine key from her pocket and started the car.

"What heaven!" she said, as they moved out of the wood towards the road. "It's almost as good as love-making."

"What is?"

"Driving this car."

"You're foolish." The red-head let her head fall

back on to the head of the seat. She closed her eyes.

Twenty minutes later, the blonde brought the great car to a standstill. "This will do, I think."

The red-head woke up. "Are we on the main road?"

"Yes. And quite near a town. Let's leave him here. But I suggest we get a train or a bus as quickly as we can."

"Shall we still go to Kiel and see Margarete?"

"I don't see what's to stop us. When they find him he'll be bound to tell them something of what happened, but I don't think he'll admit it was done by girls. He'll think of the newspapers. He's a baron and obviously rich. He's probably important enough for the thing to make quite a splash anyway. His masculine ego will keep his mouth shut about us."

"What's left of it, yes. He'll say it was men who did it."

"Anyway, we'll telephone Margarete first to make sure."

# PART TWO

## 1

Karl Gunther got out of the taxi as it stopped outside a big apartment-block in one of the residential districts of Munich. He paid the driver and looked up at his employer's windows. Lights were burning. He sighed. There had not really been much chance that she would not be at home, but he had hoped. He went into the building and crossed the lobby to the lift.

His throat was very dry and his heart was thumping as the lift stopped at her floor. Although he knew he should hurry, he walked very slowly along the richly carpeted corridor to her flat, his legs seemingly unwilling to carry him any faster. His hand stayed poised above her bell for several moments before he could summon the resolution to press it.

As usual, she opened the door herself — her maids were given the evening free whenever he was to visit her — and, as usual, he caught his breath at

41

her loveliness. Then his fear of her returned to him and he dropped his eyes.

She stepped aside to let him enter. "Good evening, Herr Gunther."

"Good evening, Fraulein Direktor," he said respectfully. He had learned that it was indispensable to treat her at all times with the full respect due to her as his employer. Once, in the middle of one of his visits, he had used her Christian name; she had made him repent it bitterly.

"You're a little late," she said. "It is unwise to be late."

"Only a very little," he said quickly. "Two minutes."

"Even so. It is unwise to be late. I thought I had already demonstrated that."

"You have, Fraulein Direktor. I'm sorry."

"I must demonstrate it again."

She led the way into the large dimly-lit living-room. She went to a cabinet containing bottles and glasses. She poured out a large glass of schnapps and handed it to him. "Your anaesthetic."

He took it from her with a small bow and drank it at a gulp. Then he began to take off his clothes.

She poured a smaller glass for herself and sipped it while she watched him undress. He folded his clothes and placed them neatly over the back of a chair. When he was quite naked he turned and stood, quite motionlessly, in front of her. His eyes held an expression of strong fear.

She regarded him with admiration, her heart beginning to beat a little faster. He was a very big man, with wide shoulders, a flat stomach and lean hips. Except where he had worn his bathing trunks, his body was deeply tanned.

"All right," she said, and handed him a key. "Go and get them."

He took the key and went to a carved cedar chest. He stooped to unlock it. He opened its lid and took out a number of whips.

"Bring everything," she said. "I'm going to give you a longer whipping tonight because I'm going away tomorrow."

He looked quickly round at her. She laughed as she saw the expression in his eyes. "Oh no," she said, "you're not going to lose your weekly whippings. I'll make up for them when I come back."

"How long will you be away?"

"Five or six weeks. So that means five or six extra whippings when I come back." She sipped her glass of schnapps. "As a matter of fact I should have gone today, but I didn't want to miss your visit this evening."

He bent over the chest and picked up a large variety of flagellation instruments. His back was covered with black, blue and red weals. On his bottom and legs were great livid bruises.

He straightened up, his arms full of the instruments, and came back to her.

"Put them on the divan," she said. "Side by side."

He turned and began to lay the various things — whips, heavy belts, a cat-o'-nine-tails, sprangers, canes, switches, birches — across the width of the divan. She moved up behind him and put her hand between his legs. She caressed the tight bag of his testicles and then put her fingers round his penis. It grew large and hard at once.

"I see you're not *so* afraid of me," she said.

"I am. I most certainly am."

She squeezed the penis lightly. "*This* isn't, though. I think I'll have to whip it, too, one of these days. It's impertinent to get as hard as this."

He strained his shoulders back and stretched the

muscles of his chest as the sweet sensation ran electrically through his loins. But he did not stop laying the whipping instruments on the divan.

She let go of his penis and stood to one side, looking down at the divan. "Yes, it has become quite a nice collection, hasn't it? Now which shall I begin with this evening?" She reached for one of the whips and drew its lash through her fingers. It was a black whip, a metre long, made of rhinoceros hide. "I think this," she said, and swung it experimentally down on the seat of a chair. It hissed as it fell; it struck the damask cover of the chair with a loud crack.

He jumped involuntarily at the two sounds, and felt his bones turn to water. He laid the last birch on the divan and stood erect. He turned to her slowly.

"It's no use begging you, Fraulein Dir—"

"None whatsoever," she said shortly. "Go and get my boots and black cape."

As he left the room she began to take off her own clothes. He went into her bedroom and opened her wardrobe. He took out a pair of high black leather boots and a floor-length black rubber cape. He ran his hand over the smooth, cool material, remembering the shock he had had when, during his first whipping, he had asked her why she wore them. "I wear the boots," she had replied, looking him in the eyes with cruelty in her own, "because they look brutal —and when I *feel* brutal they match my mood. As for the cape, I prefer to be naked when I whip someone, but I don't like his blood spattering all over my body. And I shall give you an extra twenty lashes for asking personal questions."

He went back to the living room now with the boots in one hand and the cape in the other, its cool rubber folds touching his naked body pleasantly as he walked. She was standing where he had left her, but now she was quite naked. Again he caught his breath. She had her lovely head tilted slightly to one side and her ash-blond hair caught and played with the light from the table-lamp beside her. She was of medium height, with large firm breasts on her well-shaped torso. She had a very small waist, which was the envy of her friends and of all the women who worked for her in the Munich publishing house which she had inherited the previous year from her father; she had slender hips, and legs of such shapeliness that her friends and employees felt something akin to despair when they allowed themselves to look at them. Men called her Munich's most beautiful woman, and fell over themselves to win her favour.

She sat down now, as he approached her, and lifted one of her legs. He put the cape over the back of a chair and knelt at her feet. He slid a boot on to the leg she had lifted. She put it to the floor and stamped lightly until her foot was comfortably home. Then she lifted her other leg. When he had shod her she stood up. She reached for the black whip. He remained in his kneeling position.

"All right," she said. "Kiss them."

He put his lips to the toes of her boots and kissed them. She lifted her whip and lashed it across his bent bottom. The tip of the whip curled round him and bit into a testicle. He gave a sharp cry.

"This is too long," she said. "Get me a shorter one."

He walked on all fours to the side of the divan and took a shorter whip. She swung the one she was holding and hit him neatly across the back of his knees. "Stay there a moment," she ordered. "You're just the right distance away now." She

45

swung the long whip again. It cut across his back
with a loud crack. He cried out with pain. She
swung again and hit him across the centre of his
buttocks. "Now come and kiss my boots again,"
she said. He shuffled back to her, his features
contorted, and held the shorter whip up to her.
Then he put his lips down to her boots again. He
kissed the left one, and then the right one, and
then the left one again...

"My slave!" she murmured, and lashed him hard
across his shoulders. He cried out, but he did not
stop kissing her boots.

"My abject, helpless slave!" she said. Another
lash. "My whipping-boy!" She struck him six
more times and threw down the whip. Now you
can put me in my cape."

Very slowly, with waves of pain coursing through
his body, he stood up and reached for her cape.
He slipped its long and very full folds over her
naked shoulders. She gave a little shiver as the
cold rubber fell around her. She turned round
and faced him. She took hold of his penis, now
small and soft. At her touch, it re-erected immediately.

A burning light shone in her eyes. "My whipping-
boy," she repeated softly. "My helpless whipping-
boy. He has to do whatever I tell him. He has
to come obediently and regularly for his whippings.
He has to do whatever terrible things I order him
to do. And he cringes under my whips like a
thrashed dog. He is absolutely under my thumb,
isn't he? He daren't object, he daren't refuse me
anything, and he daren't run away, dare he? He
is totally in my power, isn't he?"

She frowned as he made no answer. "*Isn't* he?"

"Yes," he said at once. "He is."

"But this" — she gave his penis a squeeze — "this

seems to like the idea of its owner being my whipping-boy. Don't you agree?"

He shook his head. "I don't think so."

"Then why does it jump whenever I touch it? Why does it become harder than a rock? I think it's because it likes you to be whipped. And so — let's get on with the whippings." She gave the penis a tug. "Come on. I'm going to tie you up to the bathroom door."

"Oh God," he murmured. "Please not that again."

"Oh yes," she said, crisply. "That again. Come on." Pulling him by his penis, she led the way to her bedroom. She stopped at a chest of drawers and opened a drawer with her free hand. She took out a length of twine, thin but very strong. She let go of his penis. "Your thumbs, please," she said.

He put his thumbs together and held them out to her. She wound the twine tightly round them several times and made a firm knot.

"I've forgotten the whip," she said. "Go and get it — the long black one."

He went back into the living-room and fetched the whip. When he returned to her, she was standing beside the door that led to her bathroom. She held three very thick books in her hands. She took the whip from him and gave him the books. "Put them down in their position."

He knelt and placed the books, one on top of the other, on the floor in front of the door. Because his thumbs were tied, he was slow and clumsy.

"Good," she said. "We're nearly ready. Now kiss me a little."

He raised his hands and opened the front of her cape. He cupped his hands round her left breast. He bent his head and put his lips to the nipple. He sucked, and played with his tongue, for a few

47

moments. Then he transferred his attentions to her right breast.

She let her head fall back. She closed her eyes. "Oh, I'm going to flog you so much tonight," she said dreamily. "I hope I don't kill you. I may, one day."

He dropped on to one knee and put his lips to her ash-blond mound. She opened her legs a little. She had begun to breathe very rapidly. He ran his tongue lightly round the edge of her mound and then licked quickly at the lips of her vagina. She gave a flinch of pleasure. He licked lightly round her mound again, and once more flicked his tongue at her vagina lips. She gave a gasp and seized his hair. She pressed his face tightly against her organs. He put his tongue slowly into her passage, withdrew it, and put it again. She began to moan softly. Her legs began to quiver.

Suddenly she pushed him away. "Enough!" she said sharply. "Get up. Go and stand on those books."

With a sigh he straightened up and moved to the bathroom door. He stepped up on the books which he had placed on the floor.

She pulled a chair up beside him and stood up on it with a swooshing rustle of her long cape. "Your hands above your head," she ordered. "High up."

He stretched his arms high above his head. His hands came to the level of a stout hook that had been fixed into the door. She took the ends of the twine that bound his thumbs and tied them tightly round the hook. With another swoosh she stepped down from the chair. "Now kick the books away," she said.

"I can't. I'm standing on them."

"Do as I say."

"I can't, Fraulein Direktor. It's impossible."

"Oh, you *are* asking for trouble!" She moved a few paces away from him and lifted the long whip. It hissed down with terrible force and cut into the flesh at the back of his knees. He screamed wildly.

"Are you going to kick them away?"

He gave a little hop and kicked with his toes. The books scattered. His body dropped, leaving him hanging by his thumbs from the book above his head. Only the tips of his toes touched the floor. He groaned.

She licked her lower lip. "That's better. Now you can be properly whipped." She regarded him thoughtfully for a moment. "I'd better gag you. The walls and doors are thick, but you're going to scream a lot, I think. I'll make certain."

She went to the chest of drawers and took out a single sheer-nylon stocking. Then she took out a pair of gossamer-like panties in black silk chiffon with lace edges. She rolled these into a tight ball and came back to the chair. With another frooshing rustle she stepped up on it again. "Open your mouth wide." She stuffed the rolled-up panties into his mouth and tied them in place with the stocking wound round the back of his neck. She stepped down from the chair, regarded him thoughtfully for a moment, and pulled the hood of her cape up over her hair.

"And now, Herr Gunther," she breathed, her chest rising and falling fast, "say your prayers." She picked up the whip and ran its lash through her fingers. She buttoned the collar of her cape. She threw its right-hand folds back over her shoulder so that her whip arm should be unhindered. With her free hand she drew its left-hand folds protectingly across the front of her body. "Say your

49

prayers," she repeated, "because the blood is really going to spatter tonight." She pressed the cool rubber against her breasts and squeezed her nipples through it. "Here come the first hundred."

She raised the long black whip, held it poised for a moment while she aimed, and brought it down across the exact centre of his buttocks with all her force. His skin broke. Blood welled up into the weal. He gave a strangled moan.

She struck again at his buttocks. The whip cut into the same weal. Its impact caused a light shower of blood to fly. Some of it spattered on to the front of her cape. Either in protest or appeal he shook his gagged head wildly.

She laughed happily. "A very good shot, that one. Right on the same place. I wonder whether I can do it again."

Her third lash missed the bleeding weal by only a centimetre or two, and created new blood of its own. Her fourth went very wide. She poised the whip again, narrowing her eyes slightly as she took careful aim. She struck, very hard. The leather hissed through the air. Her aim was very good this time. The whip fell neatly on to the wound of the first two lashes. Blood spattered again over the front of her cape and on to the polished parquet around.

She sighed deeply with pure pleasure. "I'm so glad I didn't go today. You should be very honoured. It'll make me a day late with all my plans and arrangements — and I've lost the price of my aeroplane ticket into the bargain." She lashed him across his shoulders. "You hear that?" Another lash. "That's why you should be honoured." Another lash. "*Very — very — very — very — honoured — indeed!*" She lashed with all her strength as she spoke each word.

50

Inside her body, inside her sexual organs, her excitement was raging tumultuously. She felt as though a hundred fingertips, each charged with electricity, were caressing the whole of her sexual nervous system. She knew that an orgasm was beginning to smoulder deep inside her loins; she knew that it would rise and take her in its grip at any moment if she went on with her whipping. She did not want an orgasm so quickly: she wanted to do a lot more whipping first.

She said: "I'll give you a few moments' rest. I'm going to change my whip."

She went back to the living-room. She took a newspaper and opened it wide. She laid it flat on the floor. Then she placed her long blood-wet whip upon it. She moved to the side of the divan and stood gazing down at all the other instruments that were lying there.

She sighed again and stood quite still, waiting for the raging tumult inside her to lessen a little. From the bedroom she could hear the sound of low groans. She tried not to hear them, for they excited her greatly and stimulated the tumult that had come too soon.

She stood there, her lovely head thrown back, her chest rising and falling as though she had been running. The right-hand folds of her cape were still thrown back over her shoulder, revealing the whole of the right-hand side of her lovely body. The creaminess of her skin contrasted sharply with the blackness of the rubber that covered the rest of her. Her stance, with the cape falling to the ground on her left-hand side in full, soft, graceful folds, gave her the appearance of some ethereal goddess from another world.

She felt the smoulder of her orgasm begin to lessen and recede. The tumult was raging less strongly. She knew, though, that her next lash would revive it; she would receive a sensation that would make her senses swim; it would be as though a droplet of ecstasy had been allowed to fall upon an open sexual nerve. And she would have great difficulty in restraining her mounting orgasm.

She had no patience, however, to wait any longer.

She leaned forward over the divan, studying the instruments. After some cogitation she picked up a birch made of long strips of naked whalebone.

She went back into the bedroom.


2


At this moment, five floors below, her private secretary entered the lobby of the building with a briefcase under her arm.

Erika Köstler was a very pretty girl, a slim brunette twenty-five years old. The men in the lobby turned their heads to gaze at her as she made her way to the lift. She was wearing a provocatively cut blue silk dress and shoes with high stiletto heels. She gave the impression that she was wearing nothing else. Her legs were very shapely, her waist was small, and her bosom firm. She enjoyed the knowledge that eyes were undressing her as she got into the lift.

She pressed the button of her employer's floor. She had come, ostensibly, to bring some files and papers from the office; in reality, she had come to give herself some pleasure.

Her employer, she knew, had left for Paris that afternoon for the beginning of a five-week foreign business trip, and she assumed that the maids would have been given a holiday. The flat, therefore, would be empty. She had a key to it, for one of her duties was to keep her employer's home-desk as tidy as she kept the desk at the office, and she came frequently in the evenings to do this work.

She had come one evening several weeks before, when her employer was at a dinner party, and had found the flat empty. She had seized the opportunity of inspecting more than the study in which the desk was situated. She had gone to the bedroom and opened drawers and cupboards, fingering and admiring the clothes they contained.

It was the wardrobe, however, that gave her a strong, and unexpected, thrill of delight. She had found a number of garments made of rubber — a raincoat, a negligée, a large apron, a smock, a floor-length cape, and even a pair of pyjamas.

Her thrill of delight increased as she gazed at the garments. She had a powerful fetish for any clothing that was made of rubber.

Her own wardrobe, of course, contained many similar garments, which she wore next to her skin on all possible occasions. She experienced a good deal of physical sexual excitement when she was wearing them. She experienced, in addition, a strong mental excitement whenever she saw anyone, man or woman, wearing even a simple raincoat, provided it was made of some sort of rubber. She would mentally undress the person and picture herself slipping the garment back on again over his, or her, naked body. And her heart would begin to pound...

The sight of so many different rubber things in her employer's wardrobe took her breath away. She took them out, one by one, and held them against her, letting her hand slide over the cool, silky material. It was when she took the pyjamas in her hands, light flimsy things of pale-blue rubberised silk, and realised that these at least must necessarily be worn by her employer over naked skin, that the blood went to her head and she sat dizzily on the side of the bed, her heart pounding furiously. She let herself fall slowly on her back, and pulled the garments up to her face. She breathed in the sweet, heady mixture of rubber and perfume. Her loins tingled with sexual longing.

She lay for a few moments and then stood up. She took off all her clothes. She slipped quickly into the pyjamas, shivering with pleasure as the material enveloped her. She stepped to a long mirror and regarded herself. She looked down quickly at the front of the pyjamas and frowned in puzzlement. The material was covered with many dark spots. She put a finger to one of them and scratched. It came away in a sort of dust. She shrugged her shoulders. Her employer had obviously been careless and had spilt something. The important thing now was the discovery that a very lovely woman seemed to have the same fetish as she. There was nothing she could do about it, of course; it was out of the question for her to speak of it. But it did not matter. The knowledge itself was enough. It would be very exciting, in future, working for her employer, picturing her in all these garments.

She stood for some moments more, and then, fearful lest the maids should return and find her, she took off the pyjamas, replaced them and the other things in the wardrobe, dressed herself, and left.

Tonight, she thought, as she got out of the lift, there would be no hurry. She could take off her clothes and put on all the exciting garments, slowly, one after the other, and take all the time she wanted.

She let herself into the flat and closed the door

behind her. She was surprised to find lights burning. She heard a swishing sound, and something like a human groan, from the direction of the bedroom. She paused for a second, surprised, and then walked quickly into the living-room.

She was brought to an abrupt halt by the sight of a cruel-looking whip lying curled on a newspaper on the floor. Then she saw the other instruments on the divan.

"Gott in Himmel!" she breathed. "What's going on here?"

As the sound came again from the bedroom, followed by another groan, she realised that it was the swish of some sort of whip. For a moment her impulse was to turn and run, but curiosity got the better of her. She walked on tip-toe to the open bedroom door.

Her astonishment was so great, as she took in the scene, that she could scarcely breathe. She stood at the door and watched her employer, naked under a long black rubber cape, flogging someone who was hanging from a hook in a door. His back was covered with blood and he groaned piteously as each lash struck him.

A part of her mind told her to go — to go at once, quietly and quickly. But she stood there watching, unable to move.

And at that moment her employer turned her head and saw her standing in the doorway. Her whalebone birch stayed motionless above her head for a full three seconds. Then she let it fall to her side. "What are you doing here, Erika?" she said coldly.

Erika swallowed some saliva and stammered: "I brought some papers, Fraulein Reitter. I — I'm sorry. I thought you left for Paris this afternoon."

Marlene Reitter stared at her for several moments. Then she laughed. "Yes, of course you did. I changed my mind at the last moment." She paused, and laughed again. "It's not your fault, but it's rather unfortunate that you should have come here now. I think we had better sit down and have a drink — and a talk."

Erika nodded her head quickly. "Of course, Fraulein Reitter. Anything you say." She glanced again at the man who hung from the hook. Her eyes slowly widened. "But that's — isn't that Carl Gunther from the design department?"

"It is," said Marlene. "And I think I'd better let him go home now. We shall have to have our talk. Unless" — her eyes twinkled a little — "you're a sadist, too. You wouldn't like to give him a bit of a whipping yourself?"

Erika caught her breath sharply. "There's nothing I'd like better," she said quickly.

Her employer raised her eyes. "You *are* a sadist, then?"

"No, I don't think so," said Erika. "I don't really know. I only know I'd like to give Carl Gunther a few strokes with that whip."

"Why?"

"I have a score to settle with him."

Marlene held out the birch. "Go ahead. You'll tell me about it later."

Erika took it in her right hand and gazed in fascination at its blood-drenched ends. She walked across the room to the man. "Do you know who is going to whip you now, Carl? Why don't you turn your head and look?"

He twisted his neck with difficulty and glanced at her. She saw the surprise in his eyes.

"Yes," she said. "Erika Köstler in person. With a lovely whip in her hands. You can easily understand, can't you, why she's going to whip you?" She raised the birch quickly and swung it across

56

his back. A savage thrill coursed through her. She lifted the birch again.

"Stop a moment," said Marlene, behind her. "You'd better put something over your dress. His blood is flying all over the place. You don't want to ruin it." She opened her wardrobe and took out one of the raincoats that Erika had examined a few weeks previously. It was a shimmery white thing, made of very flimsy rubber. She held it open for Erika to slip into. "This will protect it."

So, thought Erika, this is the reason why your pyjamas have those spots on them. Well, well! Aloud, she said: "Thank you very much, Fraulein Reitter. You are most thoughtful." She thrilled at the idea that Marlene Reitter was holding the garment for her. She wished she could take off her clothes before she put it on. But this was not the time. Later perhaps. Who knew what was going to happen later? Events had begun to move fast, and most surprisingly.

She slipped into the shimmery raincoat, transferring the birch from one hand to the other as she put her arms into its sleeves. She buttoned it and then belted it tightly. She lifted the birch again. She hit with all her force. The whalebone ends splayed out as they fell, and cut into a wide area of the bleeding back. "This is what I've wanted to do," she muttered breathlessly, as she lashed rapidly and repeatedly, "what I've dreamed of doing, for the last six months. Oh God, I'd like to *kill* you with this whip!"

"You may do," said Marlene, a few moments later, after another dozen lashes had fallen. "You'd better give him a rest. I've been working on him rather a lot myself."

Erika sank on to the side of the bed, panting hard.

"I'd better stop altogether," she said. "While I can. I might not be able to in a little while."

Marlene took the birch from her hand. "You must tell me all about it. But first I'll cut him down. He can rest a bit and then go home." She went into the living-room and put the birch on to the newspaper with the whip. She opened the cedar chest and took out a large sheet of plastic material. She came back into the bedroom and spread the sheet over the bed, Erika standing up as she did so. "Thank you," she said. "I've got to put this down for him to lie on. He'll really destroy the whole of the bed otherwise." She glanced at the front of the raincoat Erika was wearing. "It's a good thing you put that on."

Erika looked downwards. The raincoat was heavily spattered with blood. "Oh dear," she said. "Let me go and wash it off."

"Later," said Marlene. "We'll have our talk first." She was a little fearful of the outcome of the talk, but it was clearly necessary. Somehow or other, she had to make certain that her secretary would not chatter about what she had seen. "Don't you want to take it off, though?"

"I'd rather keep it on," said Erika quickly, and added, "until I go and wash the blood off."

"All right," said Marlene. "There's a pair of scissors in the top drawer behind you. Give me them, will you?"

Erika found them and brought them to her employer. Marlene stepped up on the chair and began to cut through the twine that she had tied to the hook.

Erika gazed up at her in openmouthed wonder. She had long realised that her employer was the most beautiful woman she had ever seen, but she had never dreamed of seeing her like this, totally

58

naked under a heavenly-looking long black rubber cape. She wished she could be naked, too, under her own shimmery raincoat. She wished they could lie together on the bed, and fondle each other. She shivered a little as she thought of the whipping she would herself receive if she were to dare to express the wish — and she realised that she would not mind being whipped by so lovely a creature.

The man's body slumped heavily downwards as the twine was cut. He staggered and just prevented himself from falling. He moved his legs stiffly and painfully, and held out his thumbs as Marlene stepped down from the chair. She cut through the twine that bound them. He began to massage them gingerly. His eyes were half-shut and expressionless.

Marlene untied the stocking at the back of his head and took the panties from his mouth. "Now you can lie down."

He moved like an automaton to the side of the bed. He flopped forward on to his stomach.

"Now," said Marlene, putting an arm round her secretary's waist and leading her towards the living-room, "we can go and have a drink and a talk."

She released the girl's waist when they were inside the other room. "I'll get out of this cape and put some clothes on."

"Oh, please don't," said Erika at once. "Please keep it on. Stay as you are."

Marlene raised her eyes. "Of course — if you want. But why? I'm finished with whipping for tonight."

"Do you only wear it for whipping, Fraulein Reitter?"

"Yes, of course."

"Because of blood splashing about?"

"Yes. Whyever else?"

Erika's face fell. "Oh, nothing. I only thought—"

She wondered for a moment whether to say what she had thought. She decided she had better not — or, at least, not yet. "But please keep it on. It looks so wonderful on you."

Marlene raised her eyebrows again. "There's more in this than meets the eye. But, all right, I'll keep it on if you want. You must tell me the real reason later on. It seems we have quite a lot to talk about tonight." She put her hand to her right shoulder and pulled the folds clear. They fell, with a quick swooshing sound, into their proper position around the right-hand side of her body. With some surprise she saw Erika catch her breath. She said nothing. She went to the bar-cabinet. "What would you like to drink? Whisky? Brandy? Kirsch? I think there's everything."

"A little brandy, please."

"Straight, or with soda?"

"Straight, please."

"All right. Do sit down and make yourself comfortable." She poured brandy into two balloon glasses and returned to the centre of the room. She gave one glass to Erika, who was still standing. "Do sit down." She sat down herself in a deep armchair. The folds of her cape fell open for an instant and revealed the whole length of her lovely legs. She covered them at once.

Erika sat in another deep chair facing her. She crossed her legs, smoothing the shimmery rubber of her raincoat over her knees.

"Zum Wohl," said Marlene, raising her glass.

"Zum Wohl, Fraulein Reitter," said Erika, and took a welcome drink from her glass. Though outwardly she seemed fairly calm and possessed, she was in a turmoil of emotions and sensations. To be sitting here with her lovely employer, who was quite naked under a maddenly exciting cape,

60

to be herself wearing a beautiful raincoat whose front was spattered with blood that she had herself made fly, to have the awesome knowledge that only a few feet away from her was a divan that was literally covered with whips and other fearful-looking things, to know that on the bed in the next room was a man who had been savagely flogged both by her employer and by herself, to remember that her employer's wardrobe contained several other exciting garments made of the rubber she loved — these were things that prevented her from feeling calm and possessed in her mind. She strove, however, to keep her outward appearance as collected as she could.

Marlene sipped her drink and regarded her secretary thoughtfully. To say the least, the situation was highly annoying — and possibly dangerous. She had always been very careful with her sadistic activities because, though Munich was a very large city, she was a well-known figure in it. The needs of her publishing company enabled her to make frequent business trips abroad, and she satisfied her sadistic appetites in foreign cities where she was unknown. In Munich she restrained herself as much as she could. It had been easier for her in the past few months because Carl Gunther had fallen helplessly into her clutches, and it was safe to give him a weekly whipping, even in Munich. The circumstances of his fall into her clutches, and her resultant total power over him, ensured that he would never open his mouth outside her flat about the things that happened to him in it. Her secretary was another matter. She might well open her mouth wide about what she had seen this evening.

She put down her glass and held out a silver cigarette box. "German on the right, Virginian on the left."

Erika took a Chesterfield. "Thank you, Fraulein Reitter."

Marlene held the lighter for her. "You said you had a score to settle with him. I'm terribly interested. Do you want to tell me what it was?"

Erika nodded. "With pleasure." She took another drink. "He gave me a baby and then refused to do anything about it. I didn't expect him to marry me, or anything like that, but—"

"Good heavens!"

"What is it?"

"Nothing, now. I'll tell you later. Go on."

Erika moistened her lips. "Well, I did expect him to do *some*thing. Find out where I could get rid of it, for instance. But he refused to do anything. He said I should have it and give it to an orphanage."

"What did you do?"

"I had an abortion."

"Yes, I see." Marlene glanced at her sharply. "You said a moment ago — while you were whipping him — something about six months ago. I think I remember something. You asked me for a week off, didn't you, about six months ago?"

"Yes. It was to have the abortion. And he refused even to pay for it. So you see I had quite a score to settle with him."

"How very, very curious," said Marlene. "My own power over him is because of an abortion." She had made up her mind. For some time she had been wondering whether to try to spin some plausible tale to her secretary, and hope for the best. Now she decided to tell her the whole truth — and still hope for the best. There would be a good deal more hope, however, since her secretary was not likely to have any sympathy for Gunther in anything concerning an abortion. "Do you

62

remember a girl called Fuchs? Elise Fuchs. She was in the design department, too."

"Yes, of course. She died, didn't she, some months ago?"

"She did."

"Peritonitis, wasn't it?"

"No. She died of an infection that followed an abortion. It was given out as peritonitis — that is to say, the doctor signed the certificate to say it was peritonitis. But it wasn't."

"Do go on. How does Gunther come into it? Did he arrange it — the abortion, I mean?"

"He did it."

Erika stared. "He did it? He did the abortion? Himself? You can't mean it!"

"I do," said Marlene seriously. "He has some medical knowlege, you know. He started out to become a doctor, but threw it up after two years at the university. So he thought he could do an instrumental abortion himself. He did, in fact. He got rid of the baby. But he killed Elise Fuchs. You should thank your stars that he didn't do the same to you. I'm amazed that he didn't attempt it."

"My God!" said Erika softly. "One of his reasons for not helping me to find an abortionist was that he didn't trust them. He said they were never safe."

"He evidently thought he was safer — with Elise Fuchs, at any rate."

"But the doctor? The certificate showing peritonitis?"

"The doctor is a close friend. They were at the university together."

Erika took a deep breath. "And how did you find out about it?"

"Elise Fuchs sent for me. I was her employer, and she had no family. She didn't die at once,

63

you see. She told me all about it. Like you, she was very angry with Gunther. He didn't go anywhere near her after he'd done the abortion. She told me a lot of details and facts which give me now a total power over him. The infection set in soon after I saw her, and when she died I had Herr Gunther up to my office for a little talk."

"I wish I could have seen his face."

"Yes," said Marlene. "It was quite a study." She paused, and then said gently: "You see, I was born a sadist. And this gave me a new victim — a new and absolutely helpless victim." She got up and reached out her hand for Erika's glass. "Let me get you another drink." She went to the bar-cabinet and took her time pouring the brandy. She wanted to give the girl a moment or two to digest this last item of information.

Erika digested it with a blend of surprise and pleasure. She herself had felt the stirrings of sexual sadism from time to time but had done nothing about it; opportunities had been lacking. She had envied other women who, according to vague rumours, had no lack of opportunities; women like her employer: beautiful, worldly, and wealthy enough to do what they wanted. With excitement she realised that a curtain was going to be lifted for her. She was about to hear some definite facts, not vague rumours.

She said: "How wonderful, Fraulein Reitter! How marvellous! Do please tell me more. Do you whip him very often?"

"Once a week."

"Once a week! So often? Do you really? And he *has* to submit to it!"

"Exactly." Marlene gave her the glass of brandy and sat down again.

"Do you only whip him — or do you do other things? Tortures and so on?"

"Oh, many other things." Marlene laughed. "I'm a thorough-going sadist, you see. I just like to give pain."

"To men only? Or to women, too?"

"I haven't either tortured or whipped a woman yet, but I don't see why I shouldn't. I prefer men, though."

"Oh, naturally." Erika was thinking again, however, that she would not at all object to being whipped, or even tortured in other ways, by this lovely woman — provided she wore one of her rubber garments while she was doing the whipping or the torturing.

She's taking this very well, thought Marlene. She seems to be quite excited by the whole situation. I wonder whether she's a sadist herself. She could very easily be. It will be very nice if she is. I can take her with me on my trips. She said: "You seemed to get quite a pleasure from whipping Gunther just now. Was it simply revenge, or anything else? Are you, by any chance, a little sadistic yourself?"

"I don't know," said Erika, running her hand again over the shimmery rubber that covered her knees. "I think I could be. I've often thought about it, anyway. And I've read a lot of books about it. De Sade and so on."

"And you've felt that you'd like to do it?"

"Oh yes. Certainly I've felt *that*. It's just that I haven't seemed to find the way to it."

"So Gunther is the first man you've whipped, is he?"

"Yes, he's the first."

"Would you like to do it to someone else — for pure sex, I mean; not for punishment?"

65

8-5

"I'd like to, very much indeed," said Erika simply.

So that's that, thought Marlene, and thank God! If I play my cards carefully, she'll not only be safe, she'll also be a very nice little assistant. "Would you like," she said, "to come with me tomorrow on my foreign trip?"

Erika stared at her. "To Paris?"

"To Paris, and then back into Germany. I have to see Baron Franz-Rüller in Kiel on some business, but it'll be quite interesting in Kiel too. There's a Swede there called Per Petersen who is quite a masochist. And after that, London."

"Oh, Fraulein Reitter" — Erika's eyes were shining — "are you really serious?"

"Yes, very serious. I'd have taken you on other trips if I'd known you felt like this. I've always gone alone because I need privacy for what I want to do."

Erika gazed at her with awed devotion. "Do you whip and torture people when you go on your trips?"

Marlene laughed. "Of course. I can't do it here in Munich — except to our mutual friend Herr Gunther."

"How do you find them? They're men, of course. You said you haven't whipped or tortured a woman yet. Are foreign men as masochistic as German men?"

"English, American and Scandinavian men are — or perhaps not so much. No one is quite so masochistic as a German man; no one loves so much to be disciplined. But the English and the Americans run a pretty close second. And the Scandinavians aren't far behind."

"What about the French? And the Italians?"

"They're hopeless, really. One can find a masochist here and there, but it's difficult."

"How do you find them? They don't just simply

announce that they're masochists, of course. So how do you find your — your victims, as you called them a moment ago?"

Marlene sipped her drink. "There are all sorts of ways. In England, for instance — and in America and Scandinavia — they do announce it, in one way or another. All we've got to do is to put the idea into their minds."

"But how do you do that? If I'd known how to do it, I would have whipped every man who's ever made love to me."

"They've been Germans?"

"Yes."

Marlene laughed. "You poor innocent chicken! All you had to do was to show them a whip or a cane or something, and tell them to bend over."

"I wouldn't have dared. They looked so serious."

"So pompous, you mean. Dear Erika, our menfolk are very pompous in sex. But just take a whip to them and you'll see how un-pompous they become. They fall over themselves to kiss our feet."

"Good heavens! Life is going to be more interesting in the future, I can see. But foreign men — Englishmen and so on — aren't so easy, you say? What happens with them? You put the idea into their minds, you say. But how do you do that?"

"I'll show you in the next week or so."

"And do they submit to *everything* you want to do to them?

"Oh, no. Not by any means. You have to make sure they're quite helpless — tied up and gagged and so on."

"Don't they make a fuss afterwards?"

"A fuss? You mean with the police or something?"

"Yes."

"Good heavens, no! Their ego! Think of their

ego. Would they like it to be splashed over the front of a newspaper that they've been whipped and tortured by a member of the weaker — the so-called weaker — sex?"

"No, I suppose not."

"But the best thing of all is to get someone really under your thumb, and let him know what is going to happen to him before it happens."

"How do you do that?"

"I'll show you that, too. There are a number of ways."

Erika took a deep breath. "Oh, life is wonderful! Thank you for taking me, Fraulein Reitter."

"You'd better call me Marlene from now on — when we're off duty, at any rate."

Erika looked at her gratefully. "All right. Thank you — Marlene."

"Good. Now I have something to ask *you*."

"Do, please. Anything."

"Why did you want me to keep this cape on?"

Erika hesitated for only the merest second. "Because I love rubber. I love any clothing that's made of rubber."

"Sexually, of course?"

"Yes."

"It gives you a thrill to touch it?"

"Oh yes. And to feel it all over my body when I've nothing on."

"But how do I come into it. This cape isn't over *your* body?"

Erika looked at her shyly. "I — I enjoy seeing someone else wearing it, too. And when it's some-one like you" — her words came in a rush — "and when it's over her — I mean, *your* — naked body, it's all I can do to stop going crazy."

Well, well, thought Marlene, so she's a lesbian, too. She probably doesn't know it, either. There

68

seem to have been a number of men in her life up to now. But she's a lesbian, all right. And that's nice. It'll be pleasant to poke her. I'd like to whip her a little, too. I wonder how she'd take it? Better wait, though, for a bit. Aloud, she said: "You poor darling. Sitting in that raincoat over your clothes all the time. I'm so sorry. Do get undressed and wear it naked." She let the folds of her cape fall a little away from her knees.

Erika stood up at once. "Oh, yes please," she said breathlessly. She slipped out of the raincoat and began to undress rapidly. When she was quite naked she picked up the raincoat again and held it up in front of her for a moment, regarding it adoringly. "It's such a wonderful thing!" She put it slowly over her shoulders, and put her arms into its sleeves.

Marlene stood up. "Let *me* button it." She put her hands on the girl's shoulders and let them drop slowly, over the rubber surface of the raincoat, to her breasts. Lightly she caressed the firm hillocks. Then, still through the flimsy rubber, she felt for the nipples and squeezed them lightly.

Erika closed her eyes and began to breathe very fast.

"Hasn't a woman done this to you before?" said Marlene.

"No," murmured Erika, dreamily. "But it's heaven, from you."

"Why don't you do the same to me?"

"Oh yes. I'd love to." Erika, her eyes still closed, put up her hands, opened the folds of the cape, and felt for Marlene's breasts.

"No," said Marlene. "Do it through the rubber, as I'm doing."

Erika opened her eyes at once and stared at her.

"So you *do* like rubber, too? It's not only for whipping that you wear it?"

"Of course not," lied Marlene glibly. "I love the feel of it against my skin, just as you do. And I adore the smell of it, too." And *that*, she thought, should do the trick. She'll never open her mouth now.

"Oh, so do I," said Erika, huskily. How marvellously things have turned out, she thought. If only that damned man weren't in the bedroom, lying on her bed, we could perhaps go there ourselves, and lie on the bed, and fondle each other a little.

As if in answer to her thoughts, Carl Gunther appeared in the doorway from the bedroom. "Excuse me, Fraulein Director," he said quietly, seeming not to notice that the two women were almost in each other's arms. "May I take my clothes? You said I could go."

The women pulled away from each other abruptly. "I ought to whip you again," said Marlene, "for not knocking before you come into a room. But never mind. Next time. Let me see your back." She turned to Erika. "I usually do him with iodine before he goes home. I don't want him to get an infection — and rob me of my weekly pleasure."

The man turned his back to her.

Erika gave a gasp as she saw the lacerated skin, the deep weals, the half-congealed blood. For a second she felt a wave of remorse that she had been responsible for some of it. But immediately the remorse was conquered by an exciting sensation of expectation. "I should like," she said slowly, "to give him a few more strokes. May I?"

Marlene shook her head. "He'd never be able to put his clothes on. His blood is nearly dry now, you see. If you whip him again it'll all open up and it'll be morning before he can go home. No, my dear, you'll have to wait till we get to Paris."

"Paris? Even Paris? You said Frenchmen aren't very masochistic."

"They're not. But there's an Englishman who lives there who is quite a masochist."

"Oh, I see. How exciting! Will you let me whip him?"

"Of course." Marlene looked closely at the back that had been presented for her inspection. "It'll be all right, but go and get the iodine."

The man went out of the living-room, across the bedroom, and into the bathroom. He returned in a moment, holding a bottle and some cotton wool in his hands. He gave them to Marlene and turned his back on her again. She opened the bottle and poured a liberal amount of iodine on to the cotton wool. Then she began to paint his weals with it. He flinched with its sting.

When she had finished he took the bottle and the wad of cotton wool from her hands. He went back to the bathroom.

Erika chuckled. "He's well-trained."

"He ought to be, after the things I've done to him."

"Do tell me. What other things do you do? Other tortures, I mean."

Marlene laughed. "Have patience, my dear. You shall see everything, in Paris and other places."

The man came back into the room and, wordlessly, put on his clothes.

When he was dressed, he looked at Marlene. His eyes were still dull. "I may go now, Fraulein Director?"

"You may, Herr Gunther," said Marlene. "Expect a telephone call from me in about five or six weeks' time."

He bowed to her and, taking no notice of Erika,

71

walked out of the living-room towards the door of the flat. He walked slowly and very stiffly.

A pity, thought Marlene. He interrupted us too soon. Never mind, though. I'll poke her in Paris tomorrow. But what a waste! She was so much in the mood. She would have accepted anything — even a whipping.

What a pity, said Erika to herself. Things were going so well. We might have gone to the bed to fondle each other a little. And she might — she just might — have wanted to whip me a little. It would have been such heaven! Never mind. Perhaps she'll do it in Paris — or London or wherever else we're going. Oh God! I'd love to be whipped by her. Not very much, of course. But I'd love her to do it a little — particularly if she'd wear this cape while she's doing it. And it seems that she loves rubber for its own sake, thank God. And she's a sadist. So it's almost certain that she'll whip me soon, and it's just as certain that she'll be wearing something of rubber when she does it. But it's an awful pity that damned man had to interrupt us tonight.

Marlene said: "You'll have to telephone for another plane reservation."

"Don't worry, Fraul — er — Marlene. I'll do it on my way home. I'll call at the air company's office. It's open all night."

"Are you able to leave at such short notice?"

"Oh yes. Oh yes, of course."

"No parents to consult?"

"Well, I have parents — but I don't have to consult them about my movements." She smiled. "After all, I'm going on a business trip with my boss, aren't I?"

Marlene laughed. "You are, indeed. All right. Just go over to the divan and choose two or three

72

things that take your own fancy — and then take
them home and pack them in your bags. And then
I'll do the same thing."

"Will you be taking that lovely cape?"

"Oh yes, of course. And some other rubber things
that you haven't seen yet. I think you'll like them."


3


The taxi drove out of the gates of the airport and
headed for the centre of Paris.

"I'm so glad," said Erika, "that they didn't open
our bags. I was on tenterhooks, though, for some
moments. I thought that that young customs man
was going to."

"Would it have mattered?" said Marlene, settling
herself comfortably into her corner. "Have you got
something that's dutiable?"

Erika turned to her in surprise. "The whips and
things! I put them very carefully at the bottom,
under a lot of clothes, but he might have found
them if he'd opened the bag and put his hand underneath."

"Why shouldn't he have found them? They're
not dutiable."

"You mean you wouldn't mind them being seen?

Marlene laughed. "On the contrary. It's a fairly
successful way to find a victim. Perhaps not here
in France, but certainly in England and America.
I always put a whip right on the top of each bag,
and I'm very happy if they do open anything. I
have to be careful in Munich, but I'm not ashamed
of being a sadist and so I'm not ashamed of my
whips being seen — outside Munich. And if a
customs officer is at all masochistic he'll try to make
a date with me as soon as he opens my bags."

"Good heavens! Will he really?"

"If he's a masochist, he will."

"And you say it happens in England?"

"And America, and Scandinavia. Yes, it happens quite frequently."

Erika thought of the back and bottom and legs of Carl Gunther, as she had seen them the previous night. "But, surely, if one becomes too brutal — "

Marlene seemed to read her thoughts. "One doesn't usually whip anyone quite as much as we whipped Gunther last night, you know. We can't — unless he's under our thumb for some reason or other. If he becomes our victim voluntarily, because he's a masochist, we have to deal less brutally with him."

"What a pity! It's nice to be able to let go. I enjoyed myself last night."

"Oh, we get our pleasure all right, don't you worry. We always give him a good deal more than he wants, but — well, there has to be a limit."

"How can you give him more than he wants? Won't he stop you?"

"Not usually. But if there's a danger that he may, we simply tie him up and gag him."

"But — " Erika frowned. "But what happens if he won't allow himself to be tied up and gagged?"

Marlene took out her cigarette case and offered it. "You have a great deal to learn, my dear. If a man is a masochist, he usually — ninety-nine times out of a hundred — *wants* to be tied and gagged. He wants to feel helpless. He wants to feel that he is in the power of a woman — that she can do whatever she likes with him. There are different degrees of masochism, of course — just as there are different degrees of sadism. Some men are fully masochistic, both physically and mentally, and this type will accept practically anything that you want

74

to do to them. They'll submit to the most appalling tortures, and get a thrill in the midst of even the most terrible pain. But they're rather rare. About three or four in every hundred, I should say. But — "

"In every hundred of masochistic men, or ordinary men?"

"Oh, masochistic men, of course. And — "

"I'm sorry to keep on interrupting," said Erika, humbly but excitedly. "But how many men would you say are masochistic? I mean out of every hundred ordinary men, how many have any masochism at all?"

Marlene laughed. "We're getting into difficult mathematics now. It depends on nationality. Here in France probably not more than about one in a hundred. In England, America and Scandinavia — and a good many other countries, I should say, but I don't know from personal experience — anything up to twenty."

"*Twenty!* Twenty per cent! Is it possible?"

"Oh, yes, certainly. In Germany it's even more than that."

Erika was silent for a moment. "Good heavens," she said softly. "Do go on, please. You were saying that they're rather rare — those that'll submit to whatever you want to do to them."

Marlene drew on her cigarette. "Most of the others are more masochistic in their minds than in their bodies. They like a little pain, of course — but they don't like too much. But before the pain comes they like to imagine the most awful things being done to them. And after it's all over they get a terrific thrill remembering it. While it's actually happening they don't usually like it. But it's too late. It's our turn now to get our own pleasure. We've given them theirs with all the preliminaries they like so much — the threats, perhaps the tying-up and gagging — but now they have to take what's coming to them, and usually it's quite a lot. I say there has to be a limit, but nevertheless they have to take a good deal of pain."

"I see," said Erika, thoughtfully. She caught a glimpse of the Eiffel Tower as the taxi turned a corner but was too interested in what Marlene was saying to make the usual exclamation. "But then, that's that, I suppose. They're no longer masochistic after what you do to them?"

Marlene laughed again. "On the contrary. As soon as the actual physical pain is finished and behind them, the mental excitement starts all over again. It's greater now, because they can think of what we did to them. They think of it and they dream of it and they wallow in it. And so, when we're ready to do it again to them, they don't offer any resistance at all. Their mental excitement is so strong that they forget the hell of the thing itself, and they long for the whole thing to happen again."

Erika nodded her head silently. She was trying very hard not to show her own excitement. Marlene was talking as though these matters were ordinary everyday occurrences. The vague rumours about women of her class had not been exaggerations, Erika realised. She hugged herself, in her corner of the taxi, in delighted anticipation of what the future held in store for her. She had a good deal more sadism in her than she had realised. As she had told Marlene the night before, she had often thought it would be extremely pleasant to whip a man before love-making but she had never seriously considered the possibility of actually doing it. Now, things had changed; her life, it seemed, had changed. In a little while they would be in the centre of Paris, and a telephone call would be made, Marlene had told her, to a masochistic Englishman. And she, too, was going to be allowed to whip this Englishman. She hugged herself again, and felt a feverish surge of sexual, sadistic longing spread through her loins.

"This Englishman," she said. "Is he one of the three per cent who will accept anything and everything?"

"No, he's not." Marlene smiled. "You're looking forward to tonight, I can see."

"Oh, yes. Yes, yes. I'm looking forward to it terribly."

"Good. It'll be a good illustration of what I've been saying, too. He is a terrific masochist, mentally. But he can't stand much pain when the time comes."

"And you give him a lot?"

"Oh yes, quite a lot. Not so much as I give Gunther, of course — but quite a lot, all the same."

"And he always comes back for more?"

"Yes, always. He comes like lightning, as soon as I ring him. You'll see, when we get to the hotel. He'll be with us within twenty minutes. And if you look at his trousers as he comes into the room you'll see he has an erection."

"Does the same thing happen with Gunther?"

"No, it doesn't. He's not a masochist at all. The whole thing is sheer terror for him."

"That must make it more exciting for you, then."

Marlene smiled. "Yes, it does. And you have the right ideas, I can see. It's a pity you've wasted so much time."

"Thanks to you, I'm going to make up for it," said Erika simply. "Do tell me, does sex come into it, too, with you? I mean love-making? Or do you only whip them?"

"Goodness, no! Sex most certainly comes into it.

Except if I whip them too hard, and they become impotent. But that doesn't happen very often. It seems to have the opposite effect. After a whipping, a man is usually ten times more randy. That's why doctors often tell old men to get themselves whipped, if they want to regain virility in their old age."

"Yes, I've heard that, but I didn't know whether to believe it or not."

"It's true enough. It has to be inferior flagellation, of course."

Erika stared for a moment. "Inferior flagellation? What's that?"

Marlene patted her knee. "I forgot that you're still at the beginning of things. Inferior and superior flagellation are the names of the two basic types of whipping. The first can be pleasant — even for the victim, and the second is pure torture — except for the three per cent whe spoke of just now. In inferior flagellation you whip only the buttocks and the upper part of the back of the legs. Of course you let yourself go and really whip! And you go on as long as you have strength — a thousand lashes, if you can. It's the places that you whip that makes it inferior, not the force or the time or the number of lashes. In superior flagellation you whip everywhere else — the back, the shoulders, the face sometimes, the chest — and particularly the nipples, the stomach, the knees — front and back, the soles of the feet, and, if you want to be really cruel, the rod and the balls."

"O-oh!" Erika sucked in her breath. She was listening with her eyes wide open and her lips parted. "O-oh, I'd love to do that."

"You have to be careful with the balls," said Marlene judiciously. "But you can get a lot of pleasure from other parts of the body, too. Just about the only place you mustn't whip is the spot above the kidneys. Some people say the back of the neck, too, but I've never taken any notice of that."

Erika was silent and thoughtful for a moment. "Life is going to be utterly wonderful," she said. "The way my heart is racing means that I must be a lot more sadistic than I ever dreamed."

"Most women are," said Marlene. "Nearly all of us have it inside us, but not many of us do anything about it."

Except, thought Erika, women of your sort and your class, who have a better opportunity. Aloud, she said: "I'm so glad I'm your secretary, Fraulein Reitter."

"Marlene," said the other. "We're not on duty."

"All right — Marlene. Thank you. It takes a bit of getting used to."

The taxi slowed down for some lights.

Marlene leaned forward and spoke to the driver through the glass opening. "There is a large rubber store a little way up on the left. Stop there for a few moments, please." Her French was fluent but had a gutteral German note in it.

"A rubber store?" said Erika, with a quickening of her heart. "What are you going to buy?"

"Nothing that would excite you," said Marlene, smiling. "I want to get a length of solid, thick, rubber tubing. It doesn't make so much noise as a whip or the other things, and our Englishman lives in a flat with rather thin walls."

"Oh, we're not going to whip him in the hotel? You said he'll come within twenty minutes of your call. It won't be for a whipping?"

"No. The hotel knows me too well. I daren't take any chances. The walls are probably very solid, but one never knows. It's better to do it in his flat this evening."

79

Erika felt disappointed. She had been looking forward to a more immediate pleasure. "I see." A thought struck her. "What if he's not in Paris? Do you know that he is?"

"No."

"What if he's not?"

"We'll just have to find someone else."

The taxi stopped.

"May I come with you?" said Erika.

"By all means."

They got out of the taxi and crossed the pavement. Several men turned their heads and watched them going through the glass doors of the store.

Marlene stopped beside a floor-walker. "Rubber tubing, please?"

"In the basement, madame. The stairs are just here."

Erika breathed in the smell of rubber that pervaded the shop. Though it was the heavy smell of goods rather than the light, sweeter smell of garments, she found it pleasantly exciting.

Marlene read her thoughts as they walked down the stairs. "It's a pleasant smell, isn't it? There's none of the almondy smell that a raincoat has, but I like it all the same." She wondered why she bothered to tell this lie. Rubber meant nothing to her. She had put up a pretence the previous night when it was necessary to secure the silence, and therefore the devotion, of her secretary, but now there was no necessity at all.

"Oh, so do I," Erika said. "There's no smell in the world to equal rubber — particularly when it's mixed with perfume. I often wonder why the big perfumiers don't put it into a bottle."

"I doubt if they'd have much of a market."

"Oh, they *would*, Marlene! Hundreds of people — thousands, in fact — are like us."

A salesman approached them.

"I want some rubber thing," said Marlene. "Solid and thick."

"Certainly, madame. May I ask for what purpose?"

"Certainly, monsieur. It is to whip people with."

The salesman looked sharply at her, opened his mouth to laugh, and slowly closed it. "Of course, madame," he said nervously. "Will you come this way, please?"

"He's no masochist," said Marlene in German, as they followed him. "He doesn't know whether to take me seriously or not, but he wouldn't trust himself alone with me for anything in the world."

The salesman put a coil of tubing on the counter.

"No," said Marlene. "Thicker, please. About as thick as my thumb." And she held up her hand in front of his face.

The man recoiled a little, and then stooped to take another coil from beneath the counter.

"This is better," said Marlene, fingering it. "Cut me two lengths, please, of seventy centimetres."

"Seventy centimetres, madame?" he said, looking at her blankly.

"Yes. The right length for a whipping."

He gave a nervous giggle and looked away from her. After that he avoided her eyes altogether. He busied himself with the cutting and the wrapping of the tubing.

"Is one length for me?" asked Erika, as they went back upstairs.

"Of course."

The taxi took no more than another ten minutes to deposit them at their hotel in the Champs Elysées.

"What a great pleasure, Mademoiselle Reitter,"

81

8-6

said the chief reception clerk. "Welcome back to Paris. I trust you are well?"

"Very well, thank you, Monsieur Laure," said Marlene. She had a very good memory for names, and always endeared subordinates to her by making them feel they had been especially remembered.

"You have your usual suite, of course, and as soon as we had your telegram this morning we freed the room opposite for your secretary. Will you follow me, please?"

He took them up in the lift and led the way first to Erika's room. He presented it for Marlene's inspection rather than Erika's. Then he opened the door of the suite opposite. A great bowl of roses stood on the table of the sitting-room.

"How nice," said Marlene, putting her nose to them. "Thank you so much."

"It is a great pleasure to have Mademoiselle Reitter with us again," said the reception clerk, and began to fuss around the suite, opening windows, patting cushions.

At last he left them alone.

Erika looked down at the parcel she had been carrying since they left the rubber store. "May I open it?"

"Do."

She slipped the string off the corners of the paper and took out the two lengths of rubber tubing. She straightened them in her hands. They felt heavy. She put one on the seat of a chair and swung the other experimentally through the air. She felt her heart begin to race again. "It'll be terribly painful, won't it?"

"Yes. In a different way from a whip, of course. That gives a sharper pain. This gives a heavier, more bruising sort. I far prefer a whip or any of the other things but they do make so much noise.

We don't want the neighbours sending for the police."

Erika swung it backwards and forwards. "It will be wonderful! I just can't wait."

Marlene lit a cigarette and went to the telephone. She asked for a number and waited. Then she began to speak in fluent English.

"Hugh? ... This is Marlene Reitter ... Oh, very well, thank you. And you? ... About an hour ago. ... Yes, I'm looking forward to seeing you, too. Why don't you come along and have a drink? ... Yes, the same hotel, the same suite. You'll find two of us here. I've brought an assistant. ... Yes, an assistant. A very pretty girl. ... Of course an assistant for that. She's quite a sadist. I hope you're in a strong condition. You'll need to be, with two of us. ... She's my secretary. ... You ask too many questions, my dear Hugh. Just come on over and have a drink. ... All right. 'Bye." She put down the telephone and looked at her watch. "Two-thirty," she said, in German. "He'll be here in twenty minutes, you'll see."

"I knew that you could speak English," said Erika, "but I never knew you were so fluent."

"I went to school in England," said Marlene. "It was there that I first played with sadism and flagellation."

Erika glanced at her watch. "I'm dying to see what he looks like."

It was exactly ten minutes to three when his knock came on the door of the suite.

Erika went to open the door.

# PART THREE

## 1

Per Petersen sat reading the evening newspaper
in the study of his house in Kiel. He sat upright
in his chair, quite motionless, and the hand that
held his cigarette had been arrested in mid-air as
he was raising it to his mouth.

"Great God!" he murmured.

He was reading the front-page story of the hold-up,
robbery and flogging of the Baron Franz-Rüller of
Koburg-See. He came to the end of the report and
read it all over again. "Great God!" he said again.
He sat still for several moments and then rose from
his chair. He went to the fireplace and pressed
a bell-button beside it.

A manservant entered the room almost immediately.

"Is Miss Hansen upstairs?"

"Yes, sir. She is with the children."

"Ask her to be good enough to come here for a moment."

He lit a cigarette while he waited, and looked again at the report.

There was a light tap on the door and his children's governess came into the room. "You wanted me, sir?"

"Good evening, Miss Hansen. Do come and sit down. Will you have a glass of sherry with me?" He had been educated at Oxford and had acquired a number of English tastes.

Margarete Hansen sat down in the armchair facing his. She crossed her shapely legs. "Thank you very much. I'd love one." She wondered what her employer wanted this time. He frequently asked her to come to his study and he always offered her a sherry, but his reasons for asking her to come were vague. She suspected that he did so because he wanted to flirt with her. He had not, however, done so yet. His manner to her was always courteous and above reproach.

He picked up the newspaper. "Do you remember Willie Franz-Rüller?"

"Yes," she said, after a moment's thought. "Baron Franz-Rüller. He dined with you last week. I had coffee with you after dinner and met him then."

"Read this," he said, and gave her the paper, folded back to show the story. "He seems to have been in the wars."

He went to a side-table in which stood the sherry decanter. He poured the wine slowly, watching her closely out of the corner of his eyes. He particularly watched her eyes, hoping to see some flicker in them that was more than an expression of ordinary interest and surprise. But there was no flicker. She read intently, with a slight frown on her face.

He sighed. He was a masochist, and for six months

had been trying to convince himself that this girl was a sadist. From time to time he had been sure that she must be, and had been on the point of saying something which would compel her either to admit it — or deny it, and leave his employment at once. It was this thought that always stopped him. She was a very good governess, and she would be very hard to replace.

He thought now of the day he interviewed her, six months ago. After his wife's death he had advertised for a governess for his children, two girls aged nine and eleven, and a boy aged thirteen who was now at day-school and would soon be going away to boarding-school. He really wanted a French-woman, so that the children could perfect their French. He had many applicants, for he was rich and well-known, and his household was luxurious and well-staffed with servants. Among the appli-cants was a fellow-Swede, a very lovely girl of about twenty-eight, who attracted him, physically, at once. He forced himself to think of his children, however, and interviewed her with the same objectivity as he gave to all the other applicants. It was when she began to speak of punishment that he lost his objectivity.

"I should want a completely free hand," she said. "I have rather old-fashioned ideas."

"What do you mean?" he asked, his heart giving a little leap.

"The cane and the birch," she said, crisply. "A good thrashing whenever necessary."

"But my boy is thirteen."

"What has that to do with it? If he needs it, a good thrashing will do him a power of good. Toughen him up. *And* with his trousers down, too. I'd want a completely free hand."

He stared at her without speaking, his heart now racing.

"Don't you believe in corporal punishment for children?" she asked.

"I do indeed," he said quickly. "It's just that it's a little — er — unusual for a girl of your age to thrash a boy of thirteen. One usually associates that with governesses of over fifty."

She laughed. "Yes, but I don't know why. I'm probably stronger."

"You probably are," he said, feeling his penis begin to rise in his trousers. "Have you done it very often?"

"Thrashed a boy of thirteen?"

"Yes."

"Well, not of thirteen. But in my last household there was a boy of sixteen, and I had to thrash him now and again."

"With his trousers down?"

"Oh yes, of course."

He opened his mouth to ask "Why of course?" and then shut it quickly. There would be time enough to ask that, and other questions, when she was in his employment. He engaged her there and then. He asked her only one other relevant question. "Do you want me to provide the cane and the birch?"

"Oh no," she said, with a sweet smile that made him tremble, "I have everything that's necessary."

She moved in the next day and, he later learned, gave all three children an immediate thrashing with a cane "just to establish matters of discipline". It was probably not a very hard thrashing because they fell in love with her at once. On her second day he had come home early from his factory and had heard the sound of the second thrashing through the open windows of his study. He had stood listening, quivering with frustrated longing, and imagining himself in the place of whichever child was being thrashed. He wondered how she would do it to him. Would she bend him over? Or make him lie over the arms of an armchair? Or — and he caught his breath — would she make him lie face-downwards on a bed? When the sounds stopped he sent for her on some flimsy pretext, offered her a sherry, and talked to her for as long as he could, his hand in his trouser pocket squeezing his erection as often as it was decently possible to do so. And every subsequent day he returned from the factory earlier, to stand at his window and listen to the sounds of her evening thrashings. She gave them at exactly the same time each evening. She counted up the children's misdemeanours during the day, and gave a number of strokes — ranging between six and twenty — at the end of the day. He had learned to distinguish between the sound of the cane and the sound of the birch. But he had not yet seen either.

He gazed at her now, as she sat reading the story about Franz-Rüller. If she was a sadist she would surely show something. The man had been flogged terribly. The report would surely have *some* effect on her...

He carried the two glasses back to the armchairs.

She looked up at him, wondering whether he had called her down especially to show her this report, and, if so, why. The baron was not a friend of hers. She had met him only once, and then only, as it were, in the line of duty. "Poor Baron Franz-Rüller," she said.

"Yes," he said, giving her her glass, and sitting down again in his chair. "They seem to have given him a terrible thrashing."

"I wonder why."

"They were probably sadists."

"Would you think so? They probably had some grudge against him."

"Grudge? But they were robbers."

"They didn't steal his car. And it's a Rolls-Royce, it says here."

Oh dear, he thought, we're not getting anywhere. "I imagine," he said slowly, "that they were both robbers *and* sadists. They took what they could — and were wise enough not to take a car like that — and then gave themselves some sexual satisfaction with a whip."

"But are there people like that?" she said, and his heart sank. "I mean, aren't people usually sadistic towards the *opposite* sex?"

His heart lifted again at once. "Go on."

"These were men whipping a man. If they'd been women, I could... No, I'm talking nonsense."

"I'm sure you're not. Do go on." We're getting somewhere at last, he told himself. But I must be careful not to show I'm excited. "You said that if they had been women, you could... You could what?"

"Oh, nothing. Nothing at all."

He drew a breath. "Were you going to say that you could understand it?"

She glanced at him sharply. I must be very careful, she told herself. If only I could be sure that you are a masochist it would be very different. I think you are. You've given so many signs... but perhaps that's only your manner. And I don't want to lose this job.

"Well," she said, "perhaps it would be easier to understand." She watched closely to see his reaction to this remark.

His nerves gave a jump, but he covered it by putting his glass quickly to his lips. "That's most interesting," he said. "Would you tell me why it would be easier?"

"Why do you ask?"

"Oh, no special reason," he said airily. "It's an interesting point of view, that's all."

Is it? she thought. I wonder how you'd take it if I really opened my mouth. If you are a masochist as I think, you'd grovel at my feet. But if I'm wrong — oh dear, oh dear, I'd be out of the house in an instant. And this is the best job I've ever had.

"Have you ever read anything of abnormal psychology?" he asked suddenly. "Havelock Ellis, Hirschfeld, and so on?"

"No."

"They're quite interesting about this sort of thing."

"Floggings?"

"Yes."

She hesitated. "I've read some of Sade and the letters of Sacher-Masoch." She said it and regretted it. She was going a good deal too far.

Oh, he thought happily, you have, have you! Now we're really getting somewhere. "Yes," he said, to give her as much as she had given him, "so have I." And to give her a little more, he added, "And I found them disturbingly interesting."

"Disturbingly?"

"Yes, rather." He thought he had better not elaborate any more on that point yet.

She looked at him with quickened interest. Every word he was now saying was almost an open admission. But she forced herself to go on being careful. She waited expectantly for his next remark. The whole conversation was becoming quite exciting.

Shall I, he asked himself — shall I come right out into the open? You *must* be a sadist. Would you, could you, have read Sade and Sacher-Masoch otherwise? Yes, I suppose you could... But would you want to take the trousers off a sixteen-year-old boy if you weren't at least *something* of a sadist? And would you travel around from job to job with a cane and a birch in your bags if you weren't? Shall I plunge? Yes, I will. To hell with it! I've got to know, one way or another.

"Do tell me something," he began, and stopped.

"Yes?" she said, quickly.

He got to his feet. "Let's have another sherry." He took the glass from her hand and went to the side-table again.

I think, she said to herself, that you were on the point of committing yourself then. I wonder what stopped you?

He handed her her refilled glass.

There was a silence.

She sipped her sherry and then said: "You asked me a moment ago to tell you something."

"Yes."

"What was it?"

He frowned at his glass. "You use a cane and a birch on my children, don't you?"

"Yes."

"Never a whip?"

"Of course not."

"No, of course not." Why the devil had he had to say that? It threw the thing out of balance. She would be on the defensive now. He must repair it somehow.

He forced a smile. "It might do Hans a world of good."

"A whip?"

"Yes."

"Oh no! Poor little Hans!"

Damn, he said to himself, damn and blast! That's made it worse. What shall I say now? This hedging is stupid. Let me say what I want and to hell with it.

I wish, she said to herself, that you'd have some courage and say what you want to say. This is altogether too nerve-racking. Have I dropped the ball now? Should I have agreed that a whip would do Hans a world of good? It wouldn't really. Poor little Hans! A whip might do *you* a world of good, and I'd love to take one to you, you great big handsome man. But how is a girl to know whether you're a masochist or just a fellow-sadist? There's no doubt now that you are one or the other. But which, for God's sake? My job depends on my knowing that.

"Yes," he said, "poor little Hans. A whip might be too much for him at his age." He suddenly looked at her and said, slowly and deliberately: "But there's something clean and almost poetic about a whip, isn't there?"

Nearer and nearer we go, she thought. But that could have been said equally by a sadist and a masochist. Which, for the love of God, are you? She said: "I agree with you. Very clean and very, very poetic."

"I know what a cane looks like, of course," he said, realising that at last he was plunging, "but I don't know what a birch looks like. Would you please show me the one you use?"

She rose from her chair at once. "Of course. I'll go and get it."

"I'm sorry to be a trouble," he said lamely.

She gave him a dazzling smile. "It's no trouble at all." She almost ran out of the room.

As the door closed behind her, he drank his glass at a gulp. He went to the side-table and poured himself a large whisky. His heart was racing fast, and his penis was very stiff. He pressed it against

93

the corner of the side-table. What, he asked himself, shall I say when she comes back with the birch? How shall I go on? But I *must* go on. I'll never again be so close to finding out. And if she *is* a sadist, what heaven it will be! A sadist of my own in my own household. I shan't have to wait for the rare visits of Marlene Reitter, and I shan't have to go off to London every few weeks to find a flagellating prostitute.

Margarete came back into the room.

She had a cane and a birch in one hand. She shut the door with the other. She turned slowly to him, with a curious look in her eyes. She stood at the door, motionlessly, staring at him.

He threw the last vestige of caution to the winds. "Are you a sadist?"

"Are you a masochist?" she answered quietly.

"Yes." It simply had to be said. But he held his breath all the same.

"Good. I thought you were. And yes, I am a sadist."

He let out his breath. "Thank God. I thought you were, but I could never be sure."

"I've been certain — without being *really* certain — that you're a masochist." She came towards him, holding out the birch. "You wanted to see what this looks like."

He took it in his hands. It was made of a dozen or so strips of heavy pliable plastic. "I always thought a birch was made of willow branches."

"They get dry and break."

"I see."

She held out the cane. "And this is Peter."

"Peter?"

"Peter the punisher. My favourite."

He took it in his hands. It was a slender cane nearly a metre in length. He swished it experimentally through the air, wondering what to say next.

She said it for him. "Which shall I use first?"

His penis gave a great throb and became even harder. "On me?"

"Yes."

"Now?"

"Yes."

"What about the servants?"

"We can go to your bedroom."

"We can, indeed."

"So which shall I use first?"

"Are you going to use them both?"

"Yes."

He looked again at the birch, and then at the cane. "Which gives more pain?"

"I don't know. I've never been thrashed with either of theɴ."

He laughed nervously. "You *must* know. How do the children react to them?"

"They seem to be more afraid of the birch, but I never know whether they're pretending or not."

"You're teasing me now. You *must* know yourself."

She smiled. "Yes, I'm teasing you a little. The birch is the worse."

"Then let's start with the cane."

"All right. You're the employer — but once I start, *I'm* the boss. You must know that."

He hesitated.

She said quickly: "Let's have a statement of the situation. You are my employer, and I am the governess of your children. You are my boss, that is to say. I shall never forget it. But you are also a masochist and I am a sadist, and whenever we have any games of flagellation together, *I* am the boss — and you will not forget it. How about that? Do you agree?"

"I agree most willingly," he said, feeling a deep peace within him. "Let us say this. If you have not a cane or a birch or something in your hand, I am your employer and your boss. But the moment I see a cane or something in your hand I shall know that you are my boss."

"And you will obey me?"

"Yes."

"In everything I say?"

"Yes, everything."

She reached out for the cane and the birch which he was still holding. "Then take down your trousers."

"Now?"

"Now, this second."

"What about the servants?"

"Tell them you're not to be disturbed."

He smiled. "With my trousers down?"

She smiled back. "No. Do that first."

"But I thought you said we'd go to my bedroom."

"We shall, don't you worry. I just want to give you six of the best here in your own study first. Ring the bell."

He went to the fireplace and pressed the bell-button. She hid the cane and the birch under the newspaper on the armchair in which she had been sitting.

Within a minute the manservant entered the room.

Per Petersen looked at him. "I don't want to be disturbed for anything."

Margarete moved towards the door. "I'll say goodnight, sir."

"Goodnight, Miss Hansen." He watched the manservant hold open the door for her, nodded to them both, and sank down into his chair, his heart pounding furiously.

She was back in three minutes. "Did you think I'd gone for good?"

"No, I didn't think that. I knew you'd wait till the coast was clear."

She went to her chair and pulled aside the newspaper. She picked up the cane. "You'd be surprised if you knew how often I've wanted to beat you with this."

"Have you indeed? And you'd be surprised to know how many times I've stood at that window listening to you doing it to the children, and wishing I could be in their place."

"I wonder whether you'll say that in five minutes' time. Go and lock the door."

He got to his feet and went to the door. He turned the key.

She waved the cane like a flag as he turned back to her. "It's nice being the boss for a change. Take off your trousers."

"Off? Not down?"

"Off." She had meant to say "down", but she had to assert herself. "Take them right off, and your pants too. That'll do for now. Upstairs I'll have you completely naked, and I'll give you *such* a beating!"

Every word she was saying was like a sexual symphony to him. He undid his trousers, pushed them down to his ankles, pushed his pants after them, and kicked his legs free. His great erection stood out from under his shirt.

"Goodness!" she said, and took it in her hands. "What a mighty thing this is. But I'm going to knock it out of you with my cane and my birch."

"I doubt whether you can."

"We'll see. Lie down over the arms of your chair."

He turned to his chair and placed himself care-

97

fully and comfortably over its arms. She lifted his
jacket and the tail of his shirt free from his bottom.
She noticed some marks on his skin. "These are
old weals," she said. "Who gave you them?" She
had begun already to feel possessive about him.

"Oh, nobody who lives here," he said, sensing
her feeling and thinking how quaint it was that
she should so soon be jealous. "A German girl who
lives far, far away."

"Not that publishing woman from Munich?"

"Yes," he said, marvelling at female perception.
"However did you guess?"

"I knew she was a sadist the first time I met her
here."

"How?"

"I don't know how. I just knew." She ran her
hand lightly over his bottom. "So she gave you
these, did she? When was it?"

"About three months ago."

"It must have been quite a thrashing for the
weals to be showing still. What did she use?" She
put a hand beneath him and played with his penis
and testicles.

"A switch," he said, stiffening at her touch. "A
whalebone riding switch."

"Did you enjoy it?"

"So and so."

"I'll get a whalebone riding switch tomorrow,"
she said, determinedly. "I'll show you. When is
she coming again?"

"The day after tomorrow, I think."

"Oh!" She opened her mouth to say more, but
shut it abruptly. She had no right yet to be so
possessive. She would have to wait a little. "Oh,
is she indeed?"

"Yes, but you mustn't be angry about it. If I'd

known about you being a sadist I wouldn't have asked her to come."

"Is she coming especially to thrash you?"

"Dear me, no. She's coming on business to see Franz-Rüller — of all people!"

She laughed. "Is she really? That's rather rich." She gave another tweak to his penis and stood erect. "And now for six of the best. Six of my own best, at any rate. But I must have something to thrash you for. I always like to have a reason. Let me see." She stood for a moment with her lovely head on one side. "Of course! I shall thrash you for taking so long to tell me that you are a masochist. You've made me wait *so* long! Most of your thrashings in the next few days will be for that."

"The next few days! Are you going to thrash me every day, then?"

"Of course. As soon as I've thrashed the children every evening I shall thrash their father. And at any other time of the day that I can find the chanec."

A warm flood of pleasure flowed through him. Life was going to be rather pleasant. If, that was to say, he could find the strength to endure the actual thrashings. It was always the same with him. He ached for them to start, and when they were over he ached for them to happen again. While they were actually happening, however, he usually screamed for them to stop. Marlene Reitter from Munich always gagged him and took no notice. He wondered what this girl would do.

Out of the corner of his eye he saw her lift the cane.

It flashed down across his buttocks and bit into the flesh. She had hit with a good deal of strength. He gave a sharp strangled cry.

"Ssshh!" she said. "You mustn't make any noise."

She lifted the cane again, and brought it down

once more with all her force. He forced himself to make no sound, but the stroke hurt him very much.

She delivered the next four strokes very quickly, and as hard as she could. She threw down the cane and sank into her chair. "Oooh, that was nice," she breathed. "It's a long time since I was able to let myself go."

He let out his breath gradually. Waves of pain coursed through him. "You don't hit the children like that?"

"Of course not. What do you think I am?"

"A sadist."

"Yes, but not that sort of sadist. Not with children. Only with big, grown-up men like you." She put her hand beneath him again and took hold of his penis. It had lost some of its stiffness during the thrashing but now, at her touch, it re-erected at once. "Turn over on your back," she said.

"You're not going to thrash my front, are you?" He sounded nervous.

She laughed. "I most certainly am, but not now. Now, I want to put this nice hard piece of bone in my mouth. Would you like me to?"

"Yes!" he said. "Yes, please." He turned over on the arms of the chair and pulled up his shirt. His penis towered upwards.

She knelt beside the chair and put the cane on the floor. She took the birch in her right hand. "Perhaps, after all, I might warm you up a little at the same time." She laid the birch lightly over his legs, a little above his knees. "Wouldn't you like that?"

"I doubt it."

"We'll see." She leaned forward and put her lips to his penis. She put out her tongue and licked delicately at the central vein. He stiffened with pleasure. She raised her birch hand and brought the plastic strips down across his legs. He flinched, although the stroke had not been hard. She opened her mouth and took the knob of his penis between her teeth. She struck again with her birch. He flinched again, with both pleasure and pain. She slid the penis into her mouth, playing with her tongue at the vein.

He began to gasp and moan with delight. The plastic strips continued to lash across his legs, harder now, but he found the pain a blissful stimulant.

She lifted her head. "If you come now," she said, "will you be able to come again when we get upstairs?"

"Yes, I think so. After half an hour, anyway."

"Good. Let yourself come then." She put her mouth over the penis again.

When his crisis arrived, thirty seconds later, she began to lash very hard. He strained and stretched, his head bent far back towards the floor. He seized a handful of her hair with both his hands and twisted it around his fingers.

She felt the sperm ejaculate from his penis and spurt towards the back of her mouth. She swallowed slowly, savouring each drop of the bitter-sweet liquid as it travelled over the back of her tongue and down her throat. As he began to finish, and the ejaculations became less violent, she lifted her mouth a little so that she could suck the slit. She sucked strongly until no further sperm was there. Then she raised her head and sat back on her heels. She put the birch down beside the cane.

He lifted his own head and looked at her. "That was marvellous," he said. "Thank you very much indeed."

"Not at all," she smiled. "I enjoyed it myself."

"Didn't you spit out my stuff?"

She shook her head.

"You mean you swallowed it?"

"Yes," she said. "I like swallowing it. I'll do that to you anytime you want it."

He closed his eyes. "What a lot of time we've wasted."

"Yes, haven't we?" She took the cane into her hand and stood up. "And now another six of the best. Turn over again."

"Not now, for God's sake! Wait until I get a bit of sex back."

She held the cane in front of his eyes. "I have this in my hand. And we agreed that whenever I have it in my hand you will obey me in everything I tell you to do. We agreed that, didn't we?"

"Yes," he said reluctantly.

"Turn over then."

"But it'll be murder now. I haven't any sex left in me at all."

"That's why I want to do it. That's where my *pure* sadism shows itself. I don't mind at all that you get some pleasure when I thrash you. I don't mind because I know that most of it is pain. But from time to time I like to know that it is *all* pain. No pleasure at all. And that is why I shall always thrash you — and thrash you very hard indeed — immediately after you have come and, as you say, have no sex in you. So, come along. Turn over."

"You *are* a sadist, aren't you!"

"Yes. And if you want me to be relatively merciful to you now, you'll turn over at once and stop wasting time."

"Oh, all right." He turned over again on to his stomach.

She laid the cane on his legs just below his buttocks. "I'm going to hit you here," she said, beginning to breathe fast. "This first time I'm

102

going to give you only six. Other times there will be many more. Tonight I'm going to be relatively merciful."

"It's going to hurt terribly there. It's the tenderest part of the legs."

"Exactly. That's why I'm going to hit you there. They are going to be a very scientific six, too. They will all be one on top of the other. I'm a pretty good shot. I've had a lot of practice." She paused and looked at him. "You mustn't make any noise. Do you think you can control yourself, or shall I gag you."

"No, I'll be quiet. I don't want the servants running here any more than you do."

She looked about the room. "You'd better have something to bite on." She went to his desk and picked up a round ebony ruler. She brought it to him and put it in his hands. "You'd better bite on that. It may help."

He twisted his head and looked at her admiringly. "You know a great deal, don't you?"

"Yes. And one more thing. If you want us to go on with our new relationship, you must remember that you've promised to obey me. That means, now, that you must not get up until I tell you that you can. The six strokes are going to hurt you so much that you'll want to jump up and stop me. If you do that, I'll walk out of the house tonight." She watched him closely to see how he would take this empty threat. If he called her bluff she would lose the game, because she would never walk out on this job now. "Do you understand?" She put a note of authority into her voice.

"Yes," he said quietly. "I understand. I'll obey you, don't worry."

"Good," she said, with a feeling of relief. "Start biting that ruler now. Here they come."

She half closed her eyes as she took aim. Then her cane flashed down with terrible force. It cut into the soft flesh and drew blood at once.

His impulse, with the dreadful agony, was to jump off the chair and stop her going on. The pain was far too great for anyone to bear. Even if he had had his loins full of sexual urges, he would not have been able to stand it. Now, with his loins drained, it was intolerable. At the back of his mind, however, was the memory of her last words. If he disobeyed her it would be the end of everything — just as everything was at its exciting beginning. She seemed to be more of a sadist than he had bargained for, but that had to be accepted. It was certainly worth a great deal to have his own private sadist under his roof, in his employment. He had better bite this ruler and endure the agony.

The cane hit him again as all these thoughts raced through his mind. It hit exactly on the bleeding weal of the first stroke. Blood splashed up into the air and fell on the floor and carpet.

His senses swam. He could not, not, *not* endure another four of these! He heard her voice and focussed his brain on to what she was saying.

" — what the servants will say when they see all this blood! Damn and damn and damn! Why didn't I bring something to put on the floor? Oh well, next time. I'll finish you off now across your buttocks. You're lucky." She changed her aim and called on all her strength. She delivered the next four strokes very rapidly, being careful not to hit twice in the same place. Blood immediately filled each weal, but it did not splash.

These last four strokes hurt him very much, too. But in comparison with the first two across the lower, fleshy part of his legs, they were almost caresses.

She took a handkerchief out of her pocket and wiped the blood from the cane. "Be careful as you stand up," she said. "You'll make the chair all bloody otherwise."

He stood up gingerly, and looked at her in awe. "*What* a sadist!"

She smiled at him warmly. "Yes, I am. Are you sorry?"

He shook his head. As always, now that the thrashing was over, and all that was left was the brutal sting of it, he felt an upliftment — almost a regret that it was over. He looked at her standing there, the cane in one hand, a bloody handkerchief in the other, and reflected that he was very lucky. Gone now was the necessity for his trips to London, whenever he felt that he could not live another moment without being beaten by some woman or other. Now he would be beaten by this one, and if the beatings were rather more agonising than he liked he would gladly suffer them. And what a woman this one was! A lovely face, a wonderful figure, and very, very shapely legs. He wondered what she would look like without any clothes on, and suddenly realised that he would know very soon.

"Shall we go up to my bedroom?" he asked.

"Are you virile again already? What a man!"

"No, but I shall be very soon. And I want to see what you look like without your clothes."

"Speaking of clothes, we must do something about all this blood on your legs before you put your trousers on again. Have you a clean handkerchief?"

"Yes. In my trouser pocket."

She picked up the trousers and found the handkerchief. "Bend over."

He bent over, resting his hands on his knees.

She dabbed at his legs and buttocks. "It's beginning to thicken a bit. It'll stop bleeding soon."

"Until you start again upstairs. Are you going to start again?"

"Of course. I haven't really used the birch yet." She went on dabbing at the weals. "But we'll have to put something down on your bed. Some sort of waterproof stuff. Plastic or something. Have you got anything?"

"Don't tell me that you don't travel with that, too."

She laughed. "I don't, as a matter of fact. I don't expect to bring blood when I thrash children. And I didn't expect to be able to thrash you — much as I've wanted to do so, many a time."

"Have you indeed? If only I'd known!"

"Never mind. We can make up for lost time now. It's wonderful to think I have a permanent victim under the same roof."

Her words were beginning to excite him again. He felt the stirrings of sex deep down in his loins. "Let's go upstairs."

"I'll go on first. I want to look in on the children for a moment."

"Have you given the evening thrashings yet?"

"No. That's why I want to look in on them. It's only your son and heir to be thrashed tonight, though."

"What for?"

"Dirty fingernails at lunch."

"How many strokes?"

"Ten."

"Does he enjoy it? Is he a masochist, too?"

"I shouldn't be at all surprised. He seems to go out of his way to earn a thrashing." She gave a final dab with the handkerchief. "This has stopped now. You can put your trousers on again." She held out the handkerchief to him, and then changed her mind. She put it in her pocket. "I'll wash this for you." She gave the cane a final wipe with her own handkerchief and put that in her pocket too. "But what about something waterproof for your bed?"

"There's a large car-cover in the garage. I think it's made of rubber. It's certainly waterproof."

"Good. That'll do wonderfully. Will you get it and bring it upstairs? I wonder, though, whether we should go to your bedroom or to mine."

"Mine has double doors."

"That settles it. I'll meet you there in about a quarter of an hour." She picked up the birch and, holding both cane and birch close against her body, went to the door. She quietly unlocked it, peered outside, turned her head quickly to give him a dazzling smile, and disappeared.

As the door closed behind her, he picked up his pants and put them on quickly. It wouldn't do for anyone to enter the study now and find him in this condition. He pulled on his trousers, tucked his shirt into place, zipped the flies shut, straightened his jacket.

He gave a great sigh of fulfilment and pleasurable anticipation. He went to the side-table and poured another whisky. He sipped it, remembering the agony of the last six strokes. He found the memory very exciting. They had hurt him very terribly, but — well, he wouldn't mind receiving them again. He grinned suddenly, reflecting that he would do so quite soon now. If she had such extra-sadistic pleasure from whipping him when he was in a drained condition, it probably meant that she would do so always. Indeed, she had said so, he now remembered. What had been her words? "I shall always thrash you — and thrash you very hard indeed — after you have come and you have no sex in you. From time to time I like to know that it is *all* pain." She had added that she was going to be relatively merciful the first time. He shivered. What would she be like when she was not relatively merciful? He would very soon find out...

He put down his glass and went out of the room. He left the house by the front door and went into the garage. His legs hurt him a good deal as he walked. He took a rolled-up car-cover from a shelf. He ran his hand over the material. Yes, it was waterproof all right; it was a sort of rubberised cotton.

He thought of Marlene Reitter. She always wore something of rubber when she whipped him. She said she didn't like to let anybody's blood splash over her skin. But she had never thought of his carpets, as Margarete Hansen had. His heart warmed as he thought of her, his new boss. How wonderful it would be to live under her power, always to watch whether she had a cane or a birch in her hand!

He returned to the house, and went straight upstairs to his bedroom, the car-cover under his arm. He threw it on the bed, and quickly took off all his clothes. He went into the bathroom and had a quick shower. He was towelling himself when he heard her knock. "Come in," he called. "It's open." He heard her enter the room and turn the key in the lock of the outer door. She closed the inner door and locked that too.

"Where are you?" she called, throwing her cane and birch on the bed.

"Here. In the bathroom."

She came to the bathroom door. He caught his breath. She was wearing a black chiffon négligée that gave a tantalising glimpse of her nakedness beneath. "I was terrified I'd run into one of the servants in the passage," she said.

He gazed at her. "You are very lovely."

She smiled. "You said you want to see what I look like without clothes. This négligée gives you an idea."

"It certainly does."

"That's why I was afraid of running into a servant. I ought to have put something on the top of it."

"You're here now. And perhaps you'll stay."

"All night?"

"Yes."

She shook her head. "You say that now. But when you've made love to me you'll want to sleep alone."

"I doubt it."

"I don't." She had decided, in the last quarter of an hour, that she must play all her cards well. If she played them well enough there was just a possibility that she might become more than merely the governess of his children. "We'll see, anyway."

He finished towelling himself and came close to her. He put his arms around her waist, his hands on her buttocks, and pulled her closely to him.

She felt his penis like a piece of wood against her mound. She began to feel very sexy. She wanted to be put down on the bed and used roughly. But, before that, she wanted to thrash him again — thrash him, this time, really hard. She wanted to lay her birch across his broad, muscular shoulders, and make him cry out. To make a man cry out under her cane or birch — or any other instrument — was a very great pleasure to her. She exulted in the feeling of power that such a cry proved she possessed — and she lashed harder in order to hear it repeated.

"Come on," she said. "Come and be thrashed again." She pulled herself away from him and turned into the bedroom. She went to the bed and looked at the car-cover. She ran her hand over its surface. "This'll do beautifully," she said. "You'd better keep it here permanently."

"Shall I spread it over the bed?"

"I will." She threw it open over the bed. It was very large and fell to the floor on all three sides. She draped some of it over the bed-head. "It may be a bit cold at first to lie on. I've put the rubber side upwards. It will be easier to wipe your blood off the rubber side."

"Are you going to be as brutal as that?" He was well aware that this was a silly question, since he had brought the car-cover from the garage for that specific purpose. He simply wanted the thrill of hearing her answer.

She herself well understood why he had asked the silly question. She gave him the answer she knew he wanted to hear. "I'm going to thrash you into strips. I'm going to make your blood run like water." She saw his eyes flash, and then half-close. I see, she said to herself. So you're more of a mental masochist than a physical one, are you? All right, I'll play along with you as much as you like. But you'll have to take a good deal of physical pain, too. *I'm* not a mental sadist — as you'll very soon find out! Aloud, she said: "That's another reason why you'll want to sleep alone tonight."

He opened his eyes. "Why?"

"You won't be able to lie on your back. You'll probably have a rather bad night — on your stomach. And you'll want to feel free to fidget."

He looked seriously at her and wondered whether things might go too far, after all. This preliminary excitement was very, very stimulating — but there seemed to be no doubt that she would do what she said she was going to do. Her delivery of six strokes downstairs, immediately after he had been drained of sex, proved it conclusively. He knew, however,

that no power on earth could now stop him; no
fear, however great, could prevent him from going
forward.  He would submit to whatever pain she
had to give him — and the knowledge that, as a
sadist, she *had* to give the pain increased his own
present mental excitement.  He would submit to it
willingly, if not gladly, in order to relive it in his
mind after it was over, to luxuriate in the pain of
sitting down — and to dream of it happening again.

"You frighten me quite a lot," he said.

She nodded.  "Yes, I know.  And you are right
to be frightened.  I am a person to be frightened
of — when I have a cane in my hand.  Or a birch
or a switch.  I'm going to buy a switch tomorrow,
as I said.  I can't have that German girl giving me
competition."

"She doesn't, you know," he said at once.

She moved closer to him and took his great penis
in her hands.  "She'd better not!" she murmured.
"But seriously, I'd like to thrash you with a switch.
A very swishy cutting one with whalebone inside it.
It could be better even than Peter the Punisher.  It
would cut more."

He caught his breath.  "I *am* afraid of you!"

"And I think," she went on slowly, "that I'll buy
a whip too.  What was it that you said downstairs?
'There's something clean and almost poetic about a
whip.'  Wasn't that it?"

"It was.  But I wonder whether I meant it."

"I'll give you an opportunity of finding out.  I'll
make you dance around your study like a performing
bear.  And I'll make you do all sorts of humiliating
things — and if you hesitate as much as a second
I'll flog you till you're unconscious."

He drew her close to him.  His heart was beating
hard.  "What sort of humiliating things?"

"I'll make you wear my underclothes.  I'll make

you put on my stockings and panties. And I'll make you put on a sanitary towel and pretend you're a woman with a period."

"Go on."

"And I'll put a padded brassière on you — one of the things the Americans call falsies."

"What else?" He was straining against her, his whole being quivering with longing.

"I'll paint your lips and your eyes. And I'll rouge your cheeks. And — and I'll do all sorts of awful things to you. And when you're like that — in that humiliated condition, I mean — I'll thrash you till you can't stand, never mind sit. You'll wish you'd never met me."

"Oooh!" He drew a great breath and quivered again from head to foot.

She drew away from him. "It's time to give you another thrashing now. Lie down on the bed." She released his penis and gave him a small push.

He turned immediately and flopped down on his stomach on the rubber car-cover. It felt very cold against his skin.

"I'm not going to tie you down now," she said, reaching for her birch. "You know the conditions, don't you? You give me complete obedience, or I leave your employment immediately." She felt quite safe now in threatening this. He had not called her bluff downstairs. That meant that he would do anything at all that she ordered him to do — on the threat of her walking out of the house. She sensed that her being a sadist, and, what was more, a sadist under his roof, in his employment, was an excitingly important thing to him — so excitingly important that she had him from now on in her total power.

"Yes," he said, "I know the conditions very well."

"What are they now at this moment?"

112

"I suppose they are" — he twisted his head and grinned up at her ruefully — "that I must not get up and stop you thrashing me."

"Exactly. Otherwise — ?"

"Otherwise you'll leave my employment." He frowned and said slowly: "I don't think you would, you know. You've found a masochist who is very convenient to you."

How right you are, she thought. But you mustn't be allowed to know it. She said: "You are very foolish. I can find a dozen masochists within an hour."

"Oh, can you?" he said lamely, and turned his head back into the pillows. "Anyway, I agree to your conditions, so there's no point in arguing about it."

"No," she said, and hit him hard across his shoulder-blades with the birch. "No, there's no point in arguing about it." She hit him again.

He gasped with the pain of her first lash, and cried out when the second cut into him.

The sound of his cry was sweet music to her ears. She hit again, very hard. "But that is not to say" — another lash — "that I shall never tie you down." Another vicious lash, this time across the small of his back.

The agony was such that he threw himself over on to his back, and held up his hands to her in supplication. "Please! Not so hard!"

"Oh, you are foolish!" she said silkily, and lashed him across his nipples. "If you prefer to be whipped across your chest it's all the same with me. Ah! I see you don't!"

He had thrown himself over on to his stomach again. "But please!" His voice was muffled by the folds of the car-cover. *"Please..."*

"Please nothing!" she answered, lashing him more

113

quickly now. "You are going to be properly thrashed tonight, and every night, and perhaps every day too." She alternated her lashes between his shoulder-blades and the small of his back. "Your life is going to be one long thrashing from now on." She paused, panting, to catch her breath. "I was saying that I may tie you down one day. And do you know how?" She put down the birch and took the cane in her hand. "One day when you do not have to go to your office —" she raised the cane and brought it down hard across the fleshy lower part of his buttocks, and felt a surge of sexual bliss as he cried out — "I shall tie you down to this bed in the early morning" — lash! lash! lash! — "and I shall give you a terrible whipping with the whip I'm going to buy" — lash! lash! lash! lash! — "the whip that is so clean and poetic as you said" — lash! lash! lash! — "and then I shall leave you for an hour or so tied down over the bed. Oh, God!" The thought of doing this to him sent the blood to her head. She stopped speaking and put all her strength into her lashes. She delivered about twenty before she stopped, and sat down on the side of the bed, exhausted and panting hard. When she regained her breath she stood up and began to cane him again, hitting very hard with every third or fourth word she spoke. "And *then*, after an *hour* or so, I shall come *back* and give you *another* terrible thrashing. And *then* I shall leave you *again* for another hour or so. And *then* I shall come *back* once more with my *whip*. And I shall *whip* you and *whip* you and *whip* you and *whip* you!" She felt the blood rising again to her head, and again thrashed for several moments without speaking. Then she went on: "And you'll stay *tied down* all day long. You won't have anything to *eat*, you won't have anything to *drink*, you won't have anything

114

to *read* or *smoke* or *do* — except watch the *clock*, which I'll leave *beside* you, and *wait* for the *whipping* which you'll receive every *hour*. And oh *God!* oh *God!* oh *God!* *Ooooh!*" She felt her senses swimming with the thought of doing all this to him, and she lashed like a girl possessed, drinking, sucking, enveloping the piteous cries which he was giving whenever he could find the breath for them.

He was in such total agony now that he could not have got up from the bed to stop her if he had wanted to. The truth was that no such thought was in his mind. He wanted to scream for her to stop, but he had no breath. The awful pain had paralysed, it seemed, even his power to speak. He could only whimper piteously. This was not the sort of pain that he enjoyed. There was nothing of sexual stimulation in these lashes. There was only breathtaking — literally breathtaking — agony. At the back of his mind he bitterly regretted having given her the newspaper story to read. That had begun it. He had given it deliberately, with the hope that it might begin something. He now saw that it had begun far too much. This would be the last time he would submit to her. Nobody, could stand sadism such as this — nobody, nobody, nobody... *When,* for God's own sweet sake, would she *stop?*

She did stop, at this moment. She stopped in sheer exhaustion, and sank down again on the side of the bed, panting convulsively. She turned her head and looked at his back and bottom, drenched in blood. She had told him that she was going to cut him into strips but she had said it more to excite him than as a serious promise. She now saw that she had indeed cut him into more strips than she had intended. She gazed at the welter of bleeding weals and sucked in her breath with satisfaction.

115

"Yes," she said, leaning forward and ruffling his hair from behind, "that was quite a good thrashing. I enjoyed it very much. Did you?"

He turned his head slowly. He opened his mouth, tried to speak, failed, swallowed, and tried again. His voice came in a croak. "Have you finished?"

"Yes. Was it nice?" She knew it could not possibly have been. He was not sufficiently masochistic — except in his mind. But she could not resist the temptation to tease him. "Did you enjoy it?"

"Don't be damned silly! Of course I didn't enjoy it."

"What a pity. I wonder why. You wanted me to thrash you, didn't you?" A quick stab of fear crossed her heart. Perhaps she had really gone too far. "Didn't you?" she repeated, ruffling his hair again.

"Yes," he said grumpily. "But not like that. Not so hard as that." He twisted himself over on his side. "Good Christ!" he said, as he saw the state of the car-cover. "Look at all this blood!" The rubber of the cover was covered with hundreds of large and small spots of blood, which had risen into the air with the lashes, and had fallen in an arc on either side of him.

"Yes," she said silkily. "Your blood. I wonder how much you've lost."

He frowned. "But seriously, you really did let yourself go, didn't you?"

She smiled. "Yes, I did. Do you mind very much? I mean, do you want to cancel our arrangement — and not do it again?"

"No," he said at once. "I don't want to cancel our arrangement." Now that the thrashing, and its immediate insufferable agony, had ended, he started to enjoy the thought and the memory of it. His

116

penis began to stiffen. She had given him a tremendous thrashing — and he had been strong enough, tough enough, to take it. "You can do it again whenever you want."

She breathed an inward sigh of relief. "That will be very often."

He lifted himself up a little and looked at what he could see of his bleeding bottom and legs. "Good Christ!" he repeated. "Tell me, what do *you* get out of this? You're a sadist, I know. But *why*? What do you get out of it?"

She put her elbows on her knees, and her head on her hands. "I'm not sure," she said slowly. "But I think it is the idea that I, a mere girl, can subjugate a member of the strong, superior sex. The lords of creation! Isn't that what men are called? Well, I have just thrashed one of them. I ordered him to lie down on his bed. I told him not to get up. I didn't have to tie him down to the bed because I knew he would obey me. You see? He, a lord of creation, would obey me, a mere girl. And he did obey me, didn't he? He lay there and took a thrashing — quite a severe thrashing — from my hand. He cried out for me to stop, but naturally I took no notice." She was silent for a moment "Yes, I think that that is the principal thing I get out of it. Power. Of course, though, I love the idea that I'm giving pain. That's why I *can* get a thrill out of thrashing a girl or a woman. I am giving them pain. And pain is *really* something clean and poetic. You said that a whip is. You are right. But it is clean and poetic because it gives such clean and poetic pain. But it is never so pleasant, so thrilling with a woman. The really great thrill comes from the total subjugation of one of the lords of creation. And when he happens to be big and strong — like you — it's quite the most sublime thrill in the world."

"I see," he said. "Yes, I think I see. But do you get anything out of ordinary sex?"

"Goodness, yes," she said. "A tremendous amount. Much more than a woman does who is not a sadist. You are going to make love to me now. And because I have thrashed you I am going to enjoy it twenty times — a hundred times — more than I would if I hadn't thrashed you. I'm all a-tingle because of what I've done to you." She put a hand to his half-erected penis. "I hope this will not let me down, though. Oh no" — it stiffened immediately at her touch — "I see it won't. Good. Move over. I'm coming." She stood up and slipped out of her negligée. She stood, naked, looking down at him.

"You're going to lie in all this blood?"

"Of course. I brought it, didn't I? I love it. It belongs to me." She lay down beside him, shivering a little at the coldness of the rubber. "I want to roll over and over in it. I want to cover my body with it." She threw herself over his back and legs, pressing him down on to his stomach and face again. She wriggled and squirmed against his lacerated flesh, pressing her mound into the blood of the weals on his bottom. She put her mouth to the weals of his shoulder-blades. She put out her tongue and ran it lightly along one of the weals. "I want to drink it," she said, taking her tongue back into her mouth and savouring the taste of the blood that had gathered at its tip. She swallowed what she could, and put out her tongue again. She ran it along another weal. "Does this hurt?" she asked, as she felt him flinch beneath her.

"Yes."

"Very much?"

"Yes."

"Good." She swallowed again. "Does it hurt as much as what caused it?"

"No, not as much as that."

"No, I suppose not. I must bring some salt up next time and rub it into you. But for now — what shall I do to give you some more pain? Oh yes, I know." She slid her hands under his chest and took hold of his nipples with her fingertips. She squeezed them hard.

He cried out at once.

His cry made her feel weak with sexual longing. She rolled off his back and lay flat. She seized his penis. "Come on," she said, pulling it roughly. "Turn over and make love to me."

He turned on to his side again and crawled on top of her. "For God's sake don't pull it like that. You'll pull it off. And then how shall I make love to you?"

She released his penis and took hold of his testicle bag. "Shall I give this a little squeeze?"

"If you do," he said seriously, "I certainly shan't be able to make love to you tonight."

She sighed, and sank her fingernails lightly into its flesh. "What a pity. All right, I won't squeeze it tonight. But I promise I'll give it such a squeezing one of these days — when I don't want you to make love to me. I'll do it the day I tie you down for the whole of the day." She guided the knob of his penis to her vagina, which was very wet. She agitated it backwards and forwards against the vagina-lips. "Don't hurry. Don't go in yet. Let me do this for a little while."

He lowered his head and took one of her nipples in his teeth. He bit it lightly. She gave a small moan of pleasure. He did the same thing to the other nipple. Then he raised his head. "Don't you want me to put something on myself? You don't want to have a baby."

"I'm quite all right," she said. "The safe period."

"I hope so."

"So do I. But we can't stop now." She gave a deep shuddering sigh and pushed his penis inside her. She put her hands up to his shoulders and gripped them hard, her nails sinking into his flesh. "Come on now. Be rough with me. Be violent. Take me."

He rammed his penis home as hard, and as far. as he could. He took hold of her hair and twisted it round his fingers, pulling her head roughly from side to side. "All right," he said between his teeth, "I'm one of the lords of creation again, eh? You need me for this sort of thing, don't you?"

He withdrew his penis and rammed again, withdrew and rammed, withdrew and rammed. He began to breathe in spasms. The memory of her thrashing filled his brain and inflamed him beyond control.

"You're going to pay for this," she gasped, in delighted satisfaction. "I'm going to give you such a thrashing when this is over, when you haven't any sex left in you at all. It will be all, all, all, all pain." Her juices gathered, and mounted. She gave a long-drawn moan of ecstasy and began, as her culmination reached its peak, to murmur: "Pain, pain, pain, pain, pain, pain..."

He rammed, withdrew, and rammed... His own culmination rose and seized him. As though from a long way off, he heard her continuing murmurs, blissful and utterly abandoned: "Pain, pain, sweet pain, delicious pain, oh pain, pain, pain..."

# PART FOUR

## 1

As Erika Köstler went to open the door of the
hotel suite she was wondering what the English
friend of her employer would look like. He was
an Englishman. Would he be a dark Celtic type
or a blond and large Saxon? She very much hoped
he would be blond and large.

She opened the door, and smiled happily. "Do
come in," she said, in English. "I'm Fraulein
Reitter's secretary." She opened the door wide and
looked at him in appreciation as he stepped into the
small hall. He was not very blond but he was very
good-looking, and he was very large indeed.

He smiled at her. "How do you do. And her
assistant, too, I think she said."

"Yes." Her heart missed a beat. "Yes, her
assistant, too."

"I'm delighted to meet you." He put his hat on

a peg and turned to the sitting-room door. "She's in here, I expect."

"Yes, do go in. She's waiting for you."

He went into the sitting-room.

"Marlene dear," he said, and opened his arms. "Welcome back to Paris."

Marlene allowed herself to be given a tremendous hug. "Hello, Hugh. You look well as usual."

"Yes," he said. "Well and strong. I'm been keeping myself strong especially for you." He looked round at Erika. "It was a good thing, I see — now that you've come armed with an assistant."

Erika looked down at his trousers. She had suddenly remembered that Marlene had said that he would have an erection when he arrived. She chuckled. It was there, plainly to be seen under his jacket, and it looked as though it was a very large one.

"What are you laughing at?" he said, glancing down at his trousers.

Erika blushed. "Oh nothing. Nothing at all."

Marlene laughed. "I told her you'd have an erection, and she was just checking. Why don't you take it out and have a better look, Erika?"

The girl hesitated. "Shall I?"

"By all means. Just unbutton him and bring it out."

"All right." She went up to him, fighting down her shyness, and opened his jacket. She put her fingers to his fly-buttons and undid them slowly, one by one. She put her hand inside his trousers and felt for the opening of his pants. She put her hand through this and took hold of his penis. It was very hard and very large — so large that she had difficulty in bringing it through the opening of the pants.

Marlene looked up at the man. "I haven't introduced you yet, have I?" She laughed. "We mustn't forget the conventions — never mind what she's doing. Mr. Hugh Lyveson and his penis — Miss Erika Köstler — "

"And her delightful fingers," he said, with a quick intake of breath.

Erika brought the penis out and gave it a little slap. "How do you do. It's very nice to meet such a large thing as this." She gave it another slap.

"Let's torture it a little," said Marlene suddenly.

"How?" said Erika.

"You'll see," said Marlene. "It's one of the things we can do to him without making any noise. Get your clothes off, Hugh."

"Oh, wait a minute," he said worriedly, although his heart had given a leap at her words. "You're not going to — "

"We most certainly are! Get undressed. This minute, do you hear. Do as I say."

He looked at her for a moment, and then began to undress. He was very quick. In little more than a minute he stood in front of them, naked.

Erika gazed in admiration at his muscular body. She moved behind him and looked at his back and bottom. There were a large number of blue-black bruises on his shoulder-blades and buttocks. H'm, she thought to herself, that must have been quite a beating. Oh, roll on tonight! I want to add my own bruises. But what are we going to do now, I wonder? What sort of torture has she in her mind?

Hugh suddenly saw the two lengths of rubber tubing, lying on the table where Erika had left them. "My God!" he said. "You're going to use that stuff again?"

"Yes, of course. Tonight though, not now."

"I wish you'd use a cane or something less heavy."

Marlene patted his cheek. "I know you would. dear Hugh. But your walls are too thin. When you move into a flat with really thick walls I'll consider using a cane."

Erika said suddenly: "Or a cat-o'-nine-tails. That would be quite light."

He glanced at her and grinned. "Oh, a blood-thirsty assistant, I see."

"Yes," said Erika demurely. "Quite bloodthirsty. But I'm looking forward, too, to using the rubber on you tonight." She could quite easily have said the tubing, but she wanted to hear herself using the word rubber. She wished she could go to her room and fetch one of her rubber garments, and put it on, and wear it for whatever torture was going to happen now. And she wished that Marlene would put on her long cloak. She said nothing, however. She would wait till the evening.

Marlene said: "Come to the bathroom, Hugh."

"Really," he protested. "Don't do that. It's a shocking torture — and I'm sure you don't get much pleasure out of it yourself."

"What nonsense are you saying now?"

"Not as much as you get from flogging, anyway."

"Perhaps you're right there. But this is going to be very pleasant for us. We'll be giving you a lot of pain. And we'll be watching you writhing in it."

"What are you going to do?" asked Erika again.

"Something very exciting," said Marlene. "Open my large bag, will you. You'll find some ropes at the bottom, on the left."

Erika opened the bag and took out the ropes. "Here they are."

"Good," said Marlene. "And just beside where they were you'll see a pair of my panties and a single stocking. We want those too."

124

Erika found the panties — black chiffon with lace edges — and the single stocking. She gave them to Marlene. She turned to Hugh and gave his penis a stinging slap with her open hand.

"You've no idea what you're going to do?" he asked.

She shook her head. "Not yet."

Marlene said: "Go and lock the door, Erika."

"I did so," Erika said. "I locked it when I let him in."

"Good. Now, Hugh, open your mouth."

He gave an elaborate sigh. "All right." He opened his mouth wide.

Marlene rolled the panties into a ball and stuffed it into his mouth. She looped the stocking over it, between his parted lips, and tied it firmly at the back of his head. "Right. We're almost ready. Come on." She took hold of his penis and led him to the bathroom. "Get in."

He stepped into the bath and stood facing the two girls. There was a light of fear in his eyes.

"Give me one of the ropes," said Marlene.

Erika handed her a length. "Can I do anything?"

"Yes. You can tie his wrists behind him with another rope." She knelt beside the bath and leaned forward to tie his feet tightly together.

"Turn round a bit," said Erika. She took another length of rope. "Put your hands behind you." She tied his wrists firmly.

Marlene glanced up. "That's very professional. Where did you learn to tie knots?"

Erika laughed. "I was a Girl Guide."

Marlene laughed with her. "The Guide Mistress would be surprised to see you now." She stood up and reached for the shower pipe. She turned on the hot tap, letting the water play over her fingers.

125

"You can guess now what we're going to do, can't you?"

Erika stood with a finger to her lips. "Yes," she breathed. "Yes, I can."

The water was getting very hot and Marlene was testing its heat carefully. Soon she could not bear her hand under it. "We begin," she said, "with his bottom. And as soon as that has been nicely scalded, we start on his front. Turn round, Hugh, and face the wall."

His eyes now were very frightened, but he obeyed her at once. Perhaps he thought that it would be unwise to make her angry.

Marlene lifted the shower pipe and let the steaming water play over his buttocks.

A strangled cry came from under his gag. He gave a jump to the end of the bath, away from the jets of the shower. Marlene turned her wrist and let the nearly boiling water follow him. He gave another strangled cry and jumped away from it again. She laughed and let the water spray downwards into the bath. "I count five," she said. "And then I give him a breather." She turned the shower on his buttocks again. "One — two — three" — he gave another jump, slipped, and crashed on to his side at the bottom of the bath. She turned the water away from him again, letting it spray against the side of the bath. "You were foolish to slip over, but you might as well stay lying down now. Turn right over, though. We want your bottom again." She handed the shower pipe to Erika, as he turned on to his stomach. "Here you are. Count five and then take it away."

Erika took the shower pipe and put her hand lightly under the spray. She drew it quickly back. The water was very hot. She moistened her lips. Her heart was thumping with excitement at the

126

thought of the pain she was going to give. She aimed the jets of water downwards at his bottom, letting the main stream fall low down on the crack between his buttocks. She began to count silently, revelling in the sound of his strangled cries and the sight of his frantic squirming about on the base of the bath.

"All right," said Marlene, as she turned the spray away from him. "Turn over again, Hugh. It's time for your front to be washed. Come on. Do you hear me. *Turn over!*"

He twisted himself slowly over on to his back. His eyes were alight with terror and supplication.

"Look," said Erika. "Look at the way he's asking us to stop!"

Marlene laughed. "Give him five seconds of heat."

"Certainly!" Erika directed the spray at his genitals. His penis was now quite soft and very small. She let the spray fall on the whole area of his testicles, penis and hairs.

He tried to twist himself away from the scalding stream but he was unable to dodge her aim, which she changed as he flung himself from side to side. He felt that an aeon passed before she lifted the spray away from him.

"He'll be nicely sterilised for tonight," she said gaily. "Shall I give him another five seconds?"

"Yes," said Marlene. "And that had better be enough."

Erika directed the water once more at the genitals, now bright red from the scald of her first application. She counted five, feeling her spirit soaring into a dizzy rapture at the sight of the torment she was giving. She moved the spray away, however, immediately she reached the number five.

Marlene turned off the tap. She leant over the

side of the bath and untied the rope around his ankles. "Get out of the bath now, Hugh."

He stood up with difficulty and stepped out on to the floor.

"Lie down on your back," she ordered. "Lie down on the floor here."

Erika raised her eyebrows.

He lay down on the cold marble of the floor. The coldness felt pleasant to the scalded skin of his bottom.

Marlene stepped up on to his chest, letting her stiletto heels sink into his flesh. "Come on," she said to Erika. "Stand up on his stomach and balls."

Erika nodded and put a foot to his stomach. She felt it harden at once as he tautened his muscles to take her weight. She stepped up on him, and felt her own stiletto heel sink into his flesh. She put her other foot to his genitals and let the sharp heel stab lightly into the bag of his testicles.

He began to make strangled noises again from beneath his gag.

"Oh," breathed Erika, "I want to whip him. *Oh, I want to whip him!*"

"Patience, my dear," said Marlene. "He's had enough pain for a little while. I think we'd better give him a drink instead. You can whip him as much as you like this evening." She stepped down to the floor. "All right, Hugh, you can get dressed again now. And I'll give you some whisky to help you recover."

2

Erika lay on the bed in her own room. Two hours had gone by since Hugh left them, and

Marlene had said that she wanted to rest for a little while.

Erika lay in a very lightweight raincoat of rubberised silk. She was naked beneath it. Occasionally she wriggled her shoulders against its silky, cool smoothness. She was feeling very, very sexy.

She began to play lightly with her vagina-lips, scratching at them with a fingernail through the shimmery material of her raincoat. She wished that she could be wearing the rubber pyjamas of her employer. She wondered whether her employer was now wearing them as she rested.

There was a knock at her door.

"Who is it?" she called.

"Marlene."

"Oh, wait a second. I'm coming." She jumped off the bed and began to take off her raincoat. Then she pulled it back over her shoulders. There was no need to hide her perversion from Marlene. She unlocked the door.

"How nice you look," said Marlene. "And you're naked underneath, I suppose."

"Oh yes, of course."

Marlene put out her hand and opened the front of Erika's raincoat. She took one of the naked breasts in her hand.

"Oh, what heaven!" breathed Erika. She caught hold of Marlene's other hand and put it to her other breast.

"Would you like us to make love?" asked Marlene.

Erika gazed at her speechlessly. She nodded her head.

"Well, let's not waste time," said Marlene, and turned to shut the door.

"Please," said Erika quickly. "Would you wear something of rubber, too?"

129

Marlene smiled. "Of course. What would you like me to wear?"

Erika was about to say "Those pale-blue pyjamas," but realised, just in time, that she was not yet supposed to know that Marlene had any pale-blue rubber pyjamas. She recovered herself and said: "Would you wear what you were wearing last night? The cloak and the boots?"

"I haven't brought the boots, but I'll wear the cloak."

"With nothing on underneath?"

Marlene laughed. "Of course. And I'll give you a little whipping, too, if you like. With one of those rubber tubes."

Erika caught her breath. "I'd love you to."

Marlene opened the door again. "Three minutes."

Erika flung herself down on her stomach over the bed. She lay for a few minutes, listening to her pounding heart. Then she stood up again and waited beside the door.

Marlene swept into the room, a rubber tube in her hand, and the long cape over her naked body. She locked the door quickly. "Have you ever been whipped before?" she asked.

"No, never."

"Have you ever wanted to be?"

"Not before last night."

"Last night? What happened then?"

"I saw you whipping Gunther, and I saw all your whips and other things — and I thought it would be wonderful to be whipped by you."

Marlene smiled. "So you're a double, are you?"

"What do you mean?"

"A masochist as well as a sadist. They're called doubles."

Erika passed her hand and elbow across her

breasts. "I don't think I'd be a masochist for anyone but you, Marlene."

"Why? A man would give you a lovely whipping — and any man would like to, I'm sure."

"Oh, no," said Erika forcefully. "Not a man. A man has to be whipped by *me*. It's from you, a woman, a beautiful heavenly woman, that I want to receive a whipping."

"You may not like it when I start. It will hurt quite a lot."

"I know."

"And you want it to hurt, do you?"

Erika nodded. "Yes, I want it to hurt."

"So there's no need to gag you. You won't cry out?"

"I'll try not to."

"I'll have to stop if you do. I don't really think we should use even this tubing on you here in the hotel, but let's give it a try. It may not make much of a noise." She looked round her, and pulled an upright chair into the centre of the floor. She sat down on it. "Come then. Lie down over my knees."

Erika felt that she was in danger of fainting from excitement as she lay down over the lap of her beautiful employer.

Marlene picked up the hem of the raincoat and pulled it clear of her bottom. She ran her hand lightly over the skin. "What a lovely little backside you have," she said, and brought the length of rubber tubing down hard across the buttocks. They gave a shudder, as though they had a life of their own. She struck again with the rubber tube.

Erika gave a gasp with each stroke but made no other sound. The pain was greater than she had expected. She put a knuckle to her mouth and pressed it against her teeth.

Marlene struck her eight more times. "That's enough for the first time. You should see you bottom. It looks as though it's got scarlet fever."

Erika clambered to her feet and went to a full-length mirror on the wall. She lifted up her raincoat and turned her back to the mirror. She twisted her head to look over her shoulder. "You're right," she said. "It's as red as a beetroot."

"It's never been whipped before," said Marlene. "That's why. But one of these days I'll whip you with something else. Something more fitting."

"A whip?"

"Yes. And a cat-o'-nine-tails. You said yourself a little while ago that a cat-o'-nine-tails would be quite light."

Erika looked at her adoringly. "Oh yes, please do."

"You little masochist! Didn't I hurt you at all just now?"

"My goodness, yes! You hurt terribly. I wanted you to stop as soon as you began. But now it's over" — she blushed shyly — "I want it to happen again."

"It will, don't you worry. Lie down on the bed now, though. Let's make love."

"How are we going to do it? Would you like me to kiss you — I mean, down there?" Erika lay down on the bed. "I've never done this before with a woman. I don't know how to start."

Marlene lay down on the bed beside her, but with her head at the opposite end. "We'll kiss each other — down there. We'll have a little soixante-neuf."

"Soixante-neuf! So that's what it means. I've often wondered."

Marlene turned over on to her side and pulled the folds of her cape away from her. She lifted the front of Erika's raincoat and bared the front of the girl's legs. She hutched herself along the bed until her mouth was on a level with the waiting vagina. "Just do whatever I do," she said, and jabbed lightly at the vagina with her tongue.

Erika stiffened at the touch, as though she had received an electric shock. She put out her own tongue and licked at Marlene's vagina.

Marlene stiffened in her turn. This is very nice, she thought. I have a very efficient secretary who is a nice little masochistic lesbian as well as a capable sadistic assistant. Things have turned out rather well.

She rounded her tongue and thrust it into the vagina passage. She reached up with her hands and took the two breasts in her grasp. With a feeling of bliss she felt Erika's tongue being pushed into her own passage, and Erika's hands feeling for her own breasts.

### 3

At about the same time, Hugh Lyveson was lying on his own bed, considering his tortures of two or three hours ago. He lay on his back, with a pillow under the small of his back to raise his scalded bottom as much as possible from the bed and so ease the pain that came from contact with the bed-clothes. He was naked, and his legs were wide open. The windows of his bedroom were also wide open, in order that the cool air might play around his scalded genitals and bring them some measure of relief.

In spite of his discomfort he felt very excited. He was, in fact, in a state of elation. He had virtually forgotten the agony of the minutes in the bath under the scalding spray, and the pain of the stiletto heels piercing his chest, his stomach, and his testicle-bag. What he remembered now was the awesome ritual of the whole thing, the horrifying yet flaming excitement of his having been so thoroughly subjugated by two lovely girls.

He put his hands to his penis, bright red and very stiff. Lightly he ran them over the inflamed skin, and revelled in the pain of his touch. He would have to put this inflamed penis into one, or both, of their vaginas within the next few hours, and he knew that it would hurt him very much. He also knew that he would relish the hurt.

It occurred to him suddenly that, since there were now two of them, one would certainly be whipping him while he pushed his penis into the other. And his bottom was equally inflamed... He would probably faint with the pain.

The thought of fainting under the pain transported him momentarily into a condition of sexual delirium. He felt his juices gathering and mounting. He ran a finger lightly up and down the central vein of his penis, the rest of his body relaxed and inert. As his juices spilled out of his penis, over his fingers, only his mind was active. He was picturing vividly the two girls. They were standing above him, whips flailing in their arms. They were flogging his scalded genitals.

4

The two girls sat on the terrace of Fouquet's, watching the phalanx of traffic that moved at an alarming speed up and down the Champs Elysées, and the crowd of sauntering Parisians, pseudo-

Parisians and foreigners that moved backwards and forwards in front of them.

"I like Paris," said Erika.

"Have you been here before?" asked Marlene.

"No, this is my first sight of it."

"Do you like it for itself, or because Hugh Lyveson is here, waiting for us to go and whip him?"

Erika laughed. "He makes Paris even more pleasant, I must admit. But I like it for itself. It's so alive."

A very pretty, and extremely well-dressed, prostitute passed in front of them for the third time.

Erika said : "Do you think she goes in for whipping, too?"

"I should think so," said Marlene. "She must, if she's good at her job."

"Not with Frenchmen, though?"

"I should doubt it. With foreigners, mainly. I should think the English are her best customers for that sort of thing."

"It's a pity that they don't know they could come to us."

Marlene smiled. "It is. I mean, it's a pity for *them*. They pay quite a lot of money, and they take a chance on whether the girl is really a sadist or not. If she's an honest business-woman — and a good actress as well — she probably makes them think that she is, but they can never be sure."

"As they could be with us," said Erika forcefully.

Marlene looked at her with amusement. "What's happened to you so suddenly? Up to last night, you didn't even know that you had any sadism in you."

"Oh, I did! I told you how I've always wanted to whip men who've made love to me."

"But you never did anything about it."

135

Erika nodded her head seriously. "That's true. I needed you, Marlene — to show me the way."

"It's a pity I didn't show it to you before," said Marlene. "However, we can make up for lost time. Kiel, tomorrow night. Did you telephone the aircompany?"

"Oh yes," said Erika, reverting suddenly to her capacity as the efficient secretary. "We're booked on the flight number 220. We leave Paris at 4.30, take off at 5.30, and we're in Kiel a little before 7 o'clock."

"We must telephone Per Petersen then, before we leave. We'll tell him to expect us about seven-thirty."

"He is your victim in Kiel?"

"Yes."

"Is he one of the three-per-cent?"

"No, he's rather like Hugh Lyveson."

"Is he as good-looking?"

"Oh yes. He's a tall, blond Swede."

"Married?"

"Was. His wife died last year."

Erika gave a sigh of contentment. "I like tall blond men. And I love the idea of thrashing them."

Marlene held up her hand to the waiter and called for a bill. "It's time for us to go and thrash one of them now."

Erika picked up the light zip-bag which she had bought at the Munich airport that morning. It contained the two lengths of rubber tubing, several pieces of rope, and two rubberised raincoats, her own and a beautiful red one of Marlene's which had been put in at her request. She put the bag on her lap and hugged it against her stomach sensually. She felt her vagina-lips open and close, open and close... "Yes," she said breathlessly. "Let's go and give him the thrashing of his life."

Hugh opened the door of his flat and stood aside for them to enter. He politely took the zip-bag from Erika's hand. He put it down on a chair in the hall.

"Oh, no," said Erika. "We want that." She put out her hand to take it again. "It's got the instruments in it."

"Yes, of course," he said, and picked it up again. He followed them into his living-room, measuring its weight as he carried it. "It's quite heavy. Whatever have you got in it?"

Marlene said: "You'll see. Get your clothes off."

"So soon?" he said. "Can't I offer you a drink first?"

"You can certainly offer us a drink, but I want you naked first. Come on, strip. Quickly!" Her voice had the crack of authority.

He put the zip-bag on the floor and began to take off his clothes.

Erika stooped, unzipped the bag, and took out its contents. She put the flimsy raincoats over the back of a chair.

"What are those for?" he asked, as he slipped off his socks. "Is it going to rain?"

Erika laughed, a little shyly. "Haven't you heard of a rubber fetish before?"

He let his trousers and pants fall to the ground. "A rubber fetish? No, I don't think so. What do you mean?"

"We like the feeling of rubber against our skin."

He looked at Marlene. "I didn't know that. You've never said anything about it before."

Marlene smiled. "You don't know *every*thing about me, my dear Hugh."

"No, of course not. Rubber, eh? I've heard of people getting quite excited about leather. But this is a new one." He went to the chair and picked up one of the raincoats. He ran his hand over its material.

"No," said Erika. "Inside. The rubber part. That's the exciting part of it."

He put his hand inside the garment. "Yes, I think I see. It's very soft and smooth."

"And cool."

"Yes, it is." He stood, feeling the material and trying to understand how a sexual fetish could be connected with it.

Erika went up to him and took the raincoat in her hands. She opened it and put its rubber surface to his bright-red genitals. She caressed them lightly through the flimsy rubber. "Does that do anything to you?"

"It hurts," he said. Her touch on his scalded skin was indeed very painful.

"Don't you find it cool and pleasant?"

"Oh yes, it's cool — and very pleasant because it's so cool. Everything is still on fire down there."

Erika sighed and took the raincoat away. She put it over the chair again. "No, you're no fetishist."

Marlene said: "He is. Not for rubber perhaps, but he's a terrific fetishist for high heels."

"So that's why you trod on him this morning?"

"Yes. He loves it — in spite of its agony."

Erika looked down at her shoes. They were not the same ones as she had worn earlier in the day, but they had very high stiletto heels too. "May I tread on him again?"

"By all means," said Marlene. "Do whatever you want. This is your party as well as mine."

Erika looked at him. He was now completely naked. "Lie down on the floor," she ordered. "Lie down on your stomach."

"Be careful," he said. "I may be a high-heel

138

fetishist as Marlene says, but I don't want to be permanently injured."

"I didn't ask what you want or don't want. Lie down."

He lay down on the carpet. His bright-red bottom was just beside her feet. She lifted one foot and put it squarely on one of his buttocks. She stepped quickly up on him and put her other foot on his other buttock. She stood unsteadily, trying to find her balance.

Marlene came beside her and put out a hand.

Erika took it and steadied herself. "Thank you. That's better." She put her weight now upon her heels and felt them press deeply into the flesh of his bottom.

"Careful!" he said quickly, turning his head sideways and trying to look up. "You will injure me terribly if you don't look out."

"You mean," said Erika, pressing harder with her heels, "that I may puncture you?"

"Yes," he said desperately. "Do be careful!"

"Do you think it would be less dangerous if I step on your back?"

"No! For Christ's sake, don't do that!"

"I want to." She lifted a foot and put it down between his shoulder-blades. She changed her balance and put her other foot beside the first. "Is that nice?"

"No! No! *No!* Please get off!"

"I think you'd better," said Marlene, quietly. "It *is* rather dangerous."

Erika stepped down to the floor at once. "All right. In any case, I'd much rather whip him."

"Let him give us a drink first."

He stood upright, a worried frown on his face. "You're not safe, you know," he said to Erika. He looked at Marlene. "She's worse than you are."

Marlene laughed. "Yes, I'm beginning to think so too. Come on, give us a drink."

"What would you like? Whisky?"

"Yes, please. With a little water."

He looked at Erika. "And you?"

"The same, please."

He picked up a box of cigarettes and offered them. Erika gave his penis a slap as she took one.

He winced.

She noticed the wince. "It's very sore, is it?"

He lit her cigarette and nodded. "Very."

She slapped it again, harder. "Good. I like to know that. I like to know that I caused it."

He lit Marlene's cigarette and went to a cupboard to get the drinks.

"Aren't you going to get undressed?" said Marlene. "And wear your nice raincoat next to your skin?"

"Yes," said Erika. "Now! Will you, too?"

"Why not?"

The two girls quickly took off all their clothes. When they were quite naked they slipped into the shimmery raincoats with a little shiver — a shiver of coldness from Marlene, a shiver of wanton lust from Erika. They tied their belts tightly.

Hugh came up to them with the glasses. "You look very nice, I must say," he remarked admiringly. "And it's nice to know that you're nude underneath." He raised his own glass. "Cheers."

"You'd better drink that down," said Marlene. "We're wasting time." She picked up the two lengths of rubber tubing and gave one to Erika. "Come on, put your glass down."

He drained the glass and put it down on a small table.

"Now bend over," she ordered. "Touch your toes."

140

"Don't be too sadistic, for God's sake," he said, as he obeyed her.

"Shut up." She raised her rubber tube and lashed hard at his inflamed buttocks. She delivered lash after lash, fast. When she had given about twenty lashes she stood aside and signalled to Erika.

Erika took her place and raised her own tube. She tried to hit harder than Marlene had done, and began to think that she was doing so as he began to utter small strangled cries. He remained in his bent-over position, however, until she let her hand fall to her side.

"All right," said Marlene. "You're warmed up now. Come into your bedroom." She led the way out of the sitting-room and into his bedroom. She switched on the lights. "You can make a little love to me now. And Erika can go on with the warming-up."

He was breathing hard as he followed her. "Give me a moment to catch my breath, please."

"No."

"At least to have another drink."

"No." She lay down on her back on the bed and opened the front of her raincoat. "Come along and make me excited."

He looked round at Erika. "Please don't hit my back with that thing."

"Why not?" said Erika sweetly.

"It's too heavy."

"So much the better. What do you say, Marlene?"

Marlene said. "Perhaps not, dear. It may make him impotent. Let him make love to me first and then we'll tie him up and really go to work on him. But hit his bottom as hard as you want." She opened her legs. "Come on, Hugh."

He put his knees on the bed and lay down carefully over her. She took hold of his penis. He winced again at her touch.

"It's going to hurt you very much, isn't it?" she murmured. "Your poor burnt little thing. It's not so little, though. It likes my hand, doesn't it — in spite of its soreness?" She guided its head towards her vagina. "But I'm so wet with the excitement of that beating that it'll be easier for you. Come along. Get in me."

Very gingerly he pushed his penis into her. The pain was excruciating — and yet exhilarating.

Erika raised her rubber tube. She swung on the balls of her feet as, with all her force, the tube descended and struck heavily into the quivering bottom.

He gasped. His penis moved forward with an involuntary movement. He felt himself being engulfed by Marlene's vagina, warm and wet. He forgot the pain of his soreness under the far greater pain that was now racking his bottom as lash after lash struck him.

"Don't be too quick," said Marlene in his ear. "You're going to get a really terrible thrashing immediately after this, in any case. But I'll double it and treble it if you're too quick. Ooo-oooh! This is heaven!" She put her hands to his back and began to scratch along its whole length with her fingernails.

# PART FIVE

## 1

Per Petersen woke late.  He was a little surprised, when consciousness came to him, to find that he was lying on his stomach.  Memory quickly came back to him and he lay inert, his head buried in the crack between two pillows, thinking of what had happened to him the night before.

As she had promised, Margarete had given him a very severe thrashing with Peter the Punisher, as she called her cane, immediately he finished making love to her.  It was a very painful thrashing because he was again drained of any sexual feeling, and he again felt he had been unwise to start these flagellatory activities with a girl who was so very much a sadist.  In his former trips to London, when he felt that his masochism had to be satisfied or he would go mad, he had always been able to stop the hand of the whipper when he had had enough, and the whipper, who was paid to give him just the amount of pleasure that he wanted, had always obeyed. With Margarete as his whipper — who whipped because she wanted to do so, and not because she was paid — there was no possibility of his cries "Stop! Stop! *Stop!*" receiving the slightest attention. She would stop when she wanted to, and not because he felt that he had had enough. When she finally threw down Peter the Punisher he had decided that this thrashing should be the last he would accept from her: her pain was too awful for anyone to endure. He was a little sulky with her, too. He did not repeat his suggestion that she should sleep the night in his bed. He wanted only to be left alone, to stretch himself out on his stomach and let sleep remove the pain that the least movement of his legs now gave him.

He fell asleep almost at once. Sometime during the night he had what would have been a nightmare for any ordinary, normal man. For him, it was a dream of great excitement. He dreamed that she took him to a torture chamber, deep beneath the ground, and strung him up to some rings that were set in the ceiling. She flogged him unmercifully, back and front, with a cat-o'-nine-tails made of wire, and then she branded her name across his buttocks with a red-hot branding-iron. Next she took a large pair of scissors and snipped off his nipples. Finally she brought a long, heavy sabre, put it to his lips, and made him kiss it. She knelt before him, put his penis in her mouth, and brought back his erection. Then she rose, stood to one side and lifted the sabre. With a strong downwards slash, she lopped off his penis. As he saw it drop, still erected, to the floor in front of him, he woke up, shuddering with terror and pleasure. He drew a deep breath when he realised it had been no more than a dream, tried to turn over, abruptly changed his mind, and went back to sleep.

Now, with daylight forcing its way through the cracks of the curtains, he lay still and considered his circumstances. His decision of the previous night to accept no further thrashings from Margarete had, of course, disappeared with his night's sleep. He looked forward to what the day, and future days, would bring. He was sure that he would be thrashed again during the coming day, and his nerves began to tingle with delighted anticipation. The only thing which did not please him so much was the realisation that he would always be thrashed after he had had any sexual fulfilment, when his body was so drained of sexual feeling that the thrashing could not give him the least pleasure. It was this type of thrashing that had made him decide, the previous night, to put a stop altogether to these new activities with his children's governess. Now, however, the idea of putting a stop to the activities was quite out of the question. He had his own private sadist under his roof — and there was no further need for his periodic trips to London. And what a sadist she was! The very fact of her insisting on thrashing him after his sexual fulfilments showed it more than anything else. In a way, he thought, it was the most exciting thing about her. It was murderous when it was happening, but — well, it was terribly exciting to think about. Perhaps he would submit willingly even to these quite murderous thrashings, too. They were part and parcel of the whole range of exciting activities. If he refused this part, she might refuse the rest of the game. She had, indeed, threatened to walk straight out of the house if he refused her anything at all. He wondered whether she had been really serious about that. He decided that he didn't dare to put

145

it to any test. He would simply do whatever she ordered him to do.

He put a hand behind him and lifted the bed-clothes away. He got out of bed slowly. He went to a mirror and looked at his weals. He was quite surprised at what he saw. Never, in all his trips to London, had he been given such weals as these.

His nerves began to tingle again.

## 2

On the other side of the house, Margarete Hansen woke up and stretched luxuriously. Her body was alive with the aliveness that comes from total fulfilment. She thought of the thrashings that she had given her employer the previous night, and she thrilled at the thought that she could repeat them whenever she had the slightest desire to do so. The only thing that she must be careful about was discretion: neither the servants nor the children must be allowed to have the least suspicion that the relationship between her employer and herself had changed since the evening before.

She looked at Peter the Punisher and her birch. They were lying on the side of her dressing-table. The room was flooded with daylight, for she never drew her curtains, and she could see the dark colour of blood on the end of them. She would have to wash them before using them again. She would, indeed, have to wash them in any case, and straight away. If any of the servants happened to see them in her wardrobe in this condition, they would think that she had been terribly brutal with one or more of the children, and this was something she did not want them to think.

She had said, she remembered, that she would

buy a whalebone switch and a whip today. She decided now that she would buy more than just these two things. But where should she buy the whips? There were plenty of shops in Kiel that sold switches for riding, but whips? It was a pity, she thought, that she was not in London. She could buy all sorts and sizes of whips there; she could even, she had heard, buy a cat-o'-nine-tails if she wanted one. She thought that the possession of a cat-o'-nine-tails would be very sweet. She would like one made of wire, not simply leather. A cat-o'-nine-tails made of wire would give a really terrible pain.

She began to feel very sadistic again. She put her hands to her breasts, underneath her silk night-dress, and caressed them as she day-dreamed. She wished that there were some deep cellar to the house which she could transform into a real torture chamber. She would have rings set in the ceiling and she would string Per Petersen up to them. She would whip him back and front with the wire cat-o'-nine-tails until he fainted. She might even keep him locked up in her torture chamber for a whole week, after having made him announce to his office and his household that he was going away somewhere for the week. She could have a burning brazier in which she could heat branding-irons, and she could brand him with red-hot irons on whatever part of his body she desired. His bottom would be a wonderful place...

She sighed, and then shook her head a little crossly. Such ideas were very stupid. They could never be put into practice. She should be satisfied — more than satisfied — with the situation as it was. She had her own personal masochist under her thumb. She could whip him whenever she wanted.

That was quite enough. She must stop these stupid thoughts of torture chambers and branding irons.

She began to consider again where she could buy a whip, or whips, in Kiel. A shop, perhaps, that sold dog-leads. Sometimes leads were made in the form of whips. Yes, that was the best idea. She would go down to Kiel immediately after breakfast.

## 3

In a small hotel in the centre of Kiel, the blonde and the red-head woke up and sent at once for a newspaper.

After leaving the Baron Franz-Rüller on the back seat of his Rolls-Royce at the side of the road, they had walked quickly into the small township, found the station, and taken the first train out. It had been going away from Kiel, but they had not minded. Their main idea was to get away from that neighbourhood as fast as they could. They had stayed on the train for an hour or so, and had got out at the small town of Sachs. They found a small hotel and, still exhausted by the violence of their activities and the subsequent fear of being arrested for them, went to bed at once. They slept late the next morning, had a leisurely lunch, and travelled back to Kiel on an evening train. They bought a newspaper at the station and read the story of the flogging, by a number of unidentified men, of the Baron Franz-Rüller.

Feeling considerably relieved, they telephoned their friend Margarete Hansen at the house of Per Petersen. They learned that she had already gone to bed. They found a small hotel in the centre of the town, registered themselves, left their ruck-sacks in their bedroom, and went out to have a late supper.

They would telephone Margarete again the next morning. And they would have another look at the next newspaper to make certain that they were still in the clear.

There was a knock on their door. A young and good-looking porter came into the room and handed the newspaper to the red-head.

"Thank you," she said. "And will you please send up two breakfasts?"

When the porter had gone she looked carefully through the newspaper. "No," she said at last, "there's nothing at all about him today. So we're quite safe."

"I'd like to take that one's trousers down," said the blonde.

"Whose?"

"That porter's."

The red-head snorted. "At this time of the morning, for God's sake!"

"What's wrong with this time of the morning? I feel fresh. And I feel randy."

"You're always randy."

"And you're always sadistic."

"Not at this time of the morning."

"I don't believe you. Wouldn't you like to give him a little whipping? Or a little penetrating with your dildo?"

The red-head frowned at her and made no reply.

"Be honest with yourself," persisted the blonde.

"Well," said the other, smiling in spite of herself, "it mightn't be altogether unpleasant. He *is* rather handsome, I must admit."

The blonde got out of bed. "Let's see what can be done about it, when he comes back with breakfast."

"*If* he comes back with breakfast. It may be a chambermaid."

149

"Then we'll send for another newspaper."

"You're quite awful. Absolutely shameless."

"So are you."

The red-head grinned. "Yes, I am. And it *is* rather a good idea — the more I think of it. In spite of being so early in the morning."

"It'll set us up for the day nicely. But I think we'd better make ourselves as enticing as we can."

The red-head got out of bed. "Yes. I think we ought to be in bras and panties. Nothing else." She went to the mirror, combed her hair, touched up her face. Then she took off her night-dress and slipped into her panties and brassiere.

The blonde followed her example. "I think he'll bring up the breakfast himself, whether there's a chambermaid for the job or not. Didn't you see the way he gave us a sort of I-wish-I-were-there-in-bed-with-you look?"

There was a knock at the door.

"We'll see now," said the red-head, and called: "Come in."

It was the young porter. He came into the room bearing a large tray and widened his eyes as he saw the two girls in their flimsy underwear. "I beg your pardon," he said. "I thought I heard you say come in."

"You did," said the blonde, shutting the door behind him. "Put the tray down there. Why do you apologise?"

He hesitated, his eyes on her naked stomach. "Er — well, I didn't know you weren't dressed, Fraulein."

"It doesn't matter to us," she said. "Does it to you? Are you shocked or something?"

"Oh no, Fraulein. Not at all."

"You don't object to seeing girls in their undies, then?"

He still stood with the tray in his hands. He frowned a little, wondering why she was teasing him. He put the tray down on a table. "No, Fraulein," he said quietly. "I like it." He felt his penis erecting.

She smiled. "I know you do."

"How?"

She nodded her head at his trousers. "I can see it there."

He blushed. "I don't know what you mean, Fraulein."

"Don't you?" she said, and went up close to him. She put her hands to his fly-buttons and undid them.

He stood as though transfixed, his eyes moving from the blonde to the red-head and back again to the blonde. He felt her cool fingers feel for, and find, his stiff penis. She pulled it out of his trousers. Then she put her hand round his testicle-bag and brought that out too.

"How would you like," she said softly, "to put me on the bed and make love to me?"

He swallowed. "I'd love it," he said, incredulously. He could not believe that this was happening to him. He glanced again at the red-head and saw that she was regarding him with burning eyes. He looked back at the blonde and wondered whether he should put his arms round her. He decided against it, and stood quite still, his genitals seeming to melt with the sensation of her cool dancing fingers.

"Tell me," said the red-head. "Are these other rooms occupied?" She nodded to the two walls of the bedroom.

"Only one is, Fraulein," he replied. "And it will be empty in ten minutes. The bags have already gone down. But why do you ask?"

"Are you prepared to pay our price?" said the blonde.

"Price, Fraulein? What do you mean?"

"Our price to allow you to make love to me, of course."

His spirits sank. He frowned. "Oh, I didn't realise."

"What didn't you realise?"

"That — that you were professionals." He was going to say prostitutes but decided to be as courteous as possible, in spite of his disappointment.

The two girls laughed together. "You must be punished a little more for that," said the red-head. "But we can assure you that we're not professionals, as you say."

"But you said something about a price."

"Yes."

He frowned again. "I don't understand. What is the price, then?"

"A dozen strokes with a whip."

His eyes opened wide. "Oh, I see," he said slowly.

"What do you see?" said the blonde, her fingers still playing lightly with his penis and testicles.

"That you're flagellants." He felt a mixture of fear and excitement. He had never been whipped by a woman but he had from time to time thought it might be rather nice.

"I'm not a flagellant," said the blonde. "*She* is."

"Well?" said the red-head. "What about it? Do you want to pay the price?"

He tried to decide quickly what to do. It might be very exciting. They were both of them extremely lovely girls. To gain time for his thoughts he said: "But what about the noise?"

"Oh dear, you're a bit stupid," said the red-head exasperatedly. "Why do you think I asked you whether these other rooms are empty or not?"

"I'm not stupid," he retorted hotly. "And all right, I'll accept your price. But I'll have to go downstairs for a minute."

"What for?"

"To pretend that I have to go out on an errand or something. I don't want them wondering where I am. How long will you take with your dozen strokes?"

"Oh, not long," said the red-head sweetly. "About a couple of minutes."

He looked back at the blonde. "And then about ten minutes with you. All right. I'll tell them I'll be out for about a quarter of an hour. But I think we'd better wait until the person next door has actually gone, hadn't we?"

"Yes," said the blonde. "You make sure that he or she, whoever it is, is safely out of the way, and then you come back here." She let go of his penis. "You'd better put that away again for the time being."

"In any case," said the red-head, "don't come back straight away. We want our breakfast first."

"Good heavens!" said the blonde, "I'd forgotten breakfast. Yes, give us a quarter of an hour at least."

The young man put away his penir and testicles, buttoned up his trousers, and left the room. He went downstairs with his pulse racing.

The red-head opened her ruck-sack, took out her whip, some cords, and her dildo and put them on the bed. Then she sat down at the breakfast table. "I'll give him the dozen first," she said, "and then I'll do him from behind while he's inside you."

"Greedy pig," said the blonde, pouring herself a cup of coffee. "You get it twice. I get it only once."

"We mustn't forget to ring Margarete when we've finished with him," said the red-head. "And I'm not a greedy pig."

153

Marlene Reitter, in Paris, was also just beginning her breakfast. She nibbled at a croissant and picked up her bedside telephone. She asked the operator to get her a Kiel number. She went on nibbling the croissant till the call came through.

"This is the Petersen residence," said a voice in German.

"I want to speak to Mr. Petersen," said Marlene.

"I'll see if he's in. Who is speaking, please?"

She gave her name and waited. After a moment Per Petersen came on the line.

"Marlene!"

"Hello, Per. How are you?"

"Very well. And you? Are you coming?"

"Yes."

"When?"

"Today. We're flying at about half-past five. We'll be in Kiel about seven."

"We?"

"I have an assistant with me this time." She chuckled at the idea of the thought that obviously came to his mind. "A very pretty assistant."

"Why are you laughing?"

"You are wondering what she assists me in."

There was a momentary pause. "Yes, what does she assist you in?"

"She's my secretary."

"Oh." His voice sounded disappointed. "Your secretary. I see."

She laughed. "Oh, Per, it's a shame to tease you. She's also my assistant in matters of whipping."

"Is she, indeed? Since when have you needed one?" His voice now showed his eager interest.

"I don't really need one, but it's fun to have one."

He hesitated, wondering whether to say it or not.

Then it came out of its own accord: "Would it be fun to have two?"

"What do you mean?"

"Would it be fun to have two assistants?"

"Who would be the other one?" Her voice sounded ominous.

"My children's governess. She's also —" And the line went dead.

"Damn!" said Marlene, and held the receiver for a moment in her hand, wondering whether to tell operator to re-connect the call. She decided not to do so. Per Petersen would expect her for dinner. He would expect two guests, in fact, for dinner. There was no need to re-connect the call. She put the receiver back on to its rest. She was frowning. She would have liked to hear what else he was going to say about his children's governess.

## 5

Per grinned as the line went dead. He wondered whether she would get through to him again. He thought it was unlikely — but it was quite certain that she would have several things to ask, and to say, when she arrived with her assistant in the evening.

He went back to the breakfast room. Margarete was at the sideboard, helping herself to a portion of bacon and eggs. She smiled at him, a warm conspiratorial smile, and said: "Good morning, Mr. Petersen. How are you this morning?"

He smiled back at her. "Very sore."

"Nice. Did you sleep well?"

"Yes. And I had a quite fantastic dream about you."

"Did you? What was it about?"

He glanced at the door to make sure that it was safely shut. "You had an underground torture chamber." He stopped as she made an exclamation. "What's the matter?"

"Nothing. I'll tell you in a moment. Go on yourself."

"You strung me up naked to some rings in the ceiling and flogged me with a cat-o'-nine-tails made of wire. Then —"

"Oh no! It's unbelievable!" She stared at him with wide-open eyes.

"You did, I assure you."

"And I branded you, didn't I?" She put the question incredulously. "With some red-hot branding irons? On your bottom?"

"Yes." It was his turn now to be incredulous. "How do you know?"

"I had the same dream. Only it wasn't really a dream — it was a sort of day-dreaming reverie."

"When?"

"When I woke up this morning."

"Mine was in the middle of the night, long before."

She turned with her plate of bacon and eggs, and sat down at the table. "There's something very curious here. Some sort of telepathy."

He helped himself to eggs and followed her to the table. "It seems like it. It's rather weird. What else was there, in your own dream?"

"Nothing else. Just the whipping with a wire cat-o'-nine-tails and the branding of your bottom. Oh yes — and keeping you locked up in the torture chamber for a week."

"Indeed? What about my work?" His penis gave an excited jump.

"It was given out that you'd had to go away for a week."

"Was it indeed? You know, you're a rather

dangerous person to have around the house, aren't you?"

She laughed. "You're more or less safe, though. There's no torture chamber deep down below this house."

No, there isn't, he thought. And it's a pity that there isn't. My God, to live with the threat of being locked up by her for a week in a torture chamber, of being branded on the bottom by her... Oh God, God! What excitement! Perhaps, though, it isn't a pity, after all. Perhaps it's a good thing. The idea is wonderful: the act might not be. It's enough that she thought of it, telepathy or not. He said: "What are your plans for this morning?"

"I'm going down to the town to buy some nice — flowers."

He glanced up as she hesitated before the word "flowers" and saw that a servant had come noiselessly into the room with fresh coffee. He waited until they were alone again. "That was quick of you. We'll have to be very careful, both of us. But what were you going to say instead of flowers?"

She glanced at the door. "Whips," she said succinctly.

"I thought it might be that," he said, as calmly as he could. He did not feel at all calm. His heart was pounding furiously. He wanted to take her, strip her, throw her to the floor, and savage her furiously.

"And a nice whalebone switch. I wish I could find a cat-o'-nine-tails, too, but that's a dream."

"A very good thing it is."

"I could get one," she said wistfully, "if I were in London."

"You're not in London. And you'll have quite enough instruments without any cat-o'-nine-tails. When are you planning to use them?"

"This evening."

157

"Oh." He suddenly remembered Marlene Reitter. "All right. You'll have company, though. The girl from Münich is coming for dinner, with an assistant."

She frowned. She was about to say something acid, and changed her mind. She was still only the governess in his house. She would have to bide her time. "That's a pity — for me, I mean. Never mind, I'll wait till she's gone. Oh no, I forgot. She's a sadist too, isn't she? She'll be going to work on you herself. You'll be in no fit condition for me afterwards. I'll wait till tomorrow." She took a deep swallow of coffee.

He considered her thoughtfully. "Why don't we make a party of it — all of us? It might be rather fun."

"Is her assistant a sadist, too?" Her voice was a little brittle.

"Yes, I understand she is."

"You haven't met her yet?"

"No."

That would make you the victim of three women with whips. Could you stand it?"

"Why not? The more the merrier."

"All right, if you want it like that," she said grimly. I'll certainly do my best to make it a very merry party. I hope you don't regret it."

6

The young porter paused at the head of the stairs. Twelve strokes with a whip. And then that blonde on the bed. But twelve strokes... Was it worth it? He paused for a moment longer and then decided that it was well worth it. After all, twelve strokes wouldn't kill him. And he *had* at times thought it would be nice to be whipped by a girl — a girl as beautiful as this red-head.

He walked to the door and knocked. He waited to hear their summons and then entered the room, closing and locking the door behind him. His eyes fell on the whip and the cords and something else on the bed, and he felt a chill of fear pass through him. He told himself again that they couldn't kill him, cruel though that whip looked.

"Fifteen minutes," he said brightly. "Here I am."

"Take off your clothes," said the red-head. She drained her cup and stood up. She took two upright chairs and placed them together. "And then lie down here." She picked up the cords from the bed. "Come along, hurry up."

He undressed himself without a word. When he was quite naked he lay down on his stomach over the seats of the two chairs.

The red-head hutched one of the chairs a little apart from the other. She indicated the crack of four of five centimetres between the two seats. "Put your rod and balls down beneath that crack."

He obeyed her in silence. He was feeling more and more frightened, but he was too dominated by her personality to protest.

She hutched the chair back again so that his genitals were tightly trapped between, and below, the seats of the two chairs. She knelt beside them and tied one of the cords around the centre legs of the chairs, making it impossible for him to wriggle his genitals loose. She moved to the other side and did the same to the other centre legs. Then she stood up and reached for the whip.

"One word of warning," she said, drawing the long leather lash through her fingers. "Don't try to pull your rod and balls free. They can't come free. They're trapped there till I undo the ropes round the chair legs. But if you try to pull yourself free, you'll castrate yourself."

"Why should I want to pull free?" he said morosely. "I'll just lie here and take your twelve."

"We'll see whether you'll just lie there," said the blonde. "You're going to want to get off those chairs as soon as she starts."

"But you'll castrate yourself," repeated the red-head, "if you try." She drew a deep breath and put a hand momentarily to her heart. As always, just before she began a whipping, it was beating furiously, almost painfully.

He twisted his head up suddenly. "Hey!" he said, excitedly. "It's my bottom you're going to hit, isn't it? Not my back."

The blonde chuckled. "It's a bit late to arrange that now."

"No!" he said, his voice shrill. "I agreed to twelve across my bottom, not my back."

"You didn't say anything about that," said the red-head. "Nor did I." She stood there in her flimsy underwear, one hand trailing the whip beside her, the other hand to her heart. Her eyes were burning with lustful cruelty. She drank in the sounds of terror in his voice. "What can you do about it now, anyway? You're absolutely at my mercy."

"No! No! Not my back! It was understood."

"Nothing was understood," she said, lifting the whip and letting its tip play lightly up and down his spine. "And even if it was, what can you do about it? I can give you a hundred across your back if I want to."

"Let me up!" he said wildly. "I want to go. I don't want to have anything to do with either of you." He pounded the floor with his fists.

She laughed, and dangled the tip of the whip in the crack of his buttocks. He reacted to this new touch as though he had received an electric shock. He gave a jerk — and immediately cried out at the pain he gave to his genitals. She laughed again. "I told you you will castrate yourself. Be careful."

"Please let me go," he said more quietly. "I'll keep my mouth shut, I promise you. I won't say anything to anybody about all this. But please let me go."

"That's very big of you. Thank you. But I don't give a damn whom you tell or don't tell." She made a loop of the whip and placed it round his neck. She stood above him and drew the loop tight. "A very good sound thrashing across your back would do you a world of good. I can see. But I'm going to give it to you across your bottom, after all. Do you know why?"

The whip was very tightly round his throat, throttling him. He made a choking noise.

She tightened the loop even more, counting the seconds in her mind. She would keep him without breath for another half minute. "Why don't you answer me? Do you want to make me angry? Do you want it across your back after all?"

He began to beat frantically again on the floor, his senses swimming.

"Careful!" said the blonde, warningly.

"He's all right," said the red-heat, and counted the last five seconds. She released her hold on the whip. He drew a great gulp of air into his lungs, swallowed, exhaled, and drew another great breath. He twisted his head up at her. His eyes were panic-stricken. "You must be a devil!" he whispered.

She swung the whip through the air. It hissed ominously. His words gave her tremendous pleasure. So did the panic-stricken look in his eyes. "I was about to tell you why I'm going to be kind and thrash only your bottom. It's because my friend

161

wants to have you afterwards, and I don't think you'd be any good for her if I whip your back. You don't seem to be very tough. For that reason I'm going to gag you." She went to where her rucksack was lying and found the stockings with which she had gagged Franz-Rüller. She rolled one of them into a ball and came back to him. "Open your mouth wide," she ordered. He opened his mouth to protest — and was quickly and efficiently gagged almost before he realised what was happening. She measured her distance with the whip at arm's length, settled herself comfortably with her feet slightly apart, put her hand once more to her heart, and drew another deep breath, a breath of quivering exhilaration. "Now!" she murmured. She raised the whip high above her head, held it there for an instant, and brought it hissing down with all her force across the centre of his buttocks.

His body gave a great flinch, but his trapped genitals prevented it from being more than a flinch. A livid weal sprang into being across his bottom. and tiny drops of blood began to gather in it.

She gave him the dozen lashes with equal force, and with a pause of some seconds between each. He groaned, choked, grunted, beat his fists upon the floor, and writhed his body as much as his genitals would let him. His noises and his desperate writhings doubled and trebled the rapture she felt at the sight of her whip cutting into his flesh. She felt herself uplifted, transported, translated into another world of stark and savage ecstasy.

The blonde watched the terrible thrashing with a light in her own eyes. She was not the sadist that her friend was, but she enjoyed watching a flogging. She counted the lashes, fearful that the red-head would not stop on the twelfth stroke. She was ready to put out her hand, to bring the thrashing to a finish. But it was not necessary. On the twelfth stroke the red-head dropped the whip beside her, tottered to the side of the bed and fell forward on to her face.

The blonde regarded the writhing man. "It's over," she said. "You've paid the price. Now you can have some reward — after you've got your breath back." She looked at his bleeding buttocks. "Oh dear, blood in bucketfuls again." I'll have to clean you up a bit. But what with?" She looked around the room. "I can't use the hotel towels, I suppose. Oh damn! I'll have to use one of ours." She went to her ruck-sack and took out a white linen hand-towel and a bottle of eau-de-cologne. "This is about ninety-five per cent alcohol. It'll sterilise you all right." She came back to him, opened the bottle, and poured the liquid over his bleeding weals. He gave another flinch as the alcohol seemed to bite him. "Sorry," she said, "but you have to be cleaned up a bit, for your own sake." She laid the hand-towel over his bottom. "That'll suck the blood up in a moment or two. And then you can start on me, can't you?"

He grunted.

She looked at him and smiled. "You're still gagged, of course. Poor boy. Here, let me undo it." She untied the stocking and took the other one out of his mouth. "There. That's better, isn't it?"

"Untie the chairs, please," he said quietly, working his tongue to produce saliva.

Something in his tone made her glance at him, with narrowed eyes. "Don't you wand to lie still and relax for a minute or two?"

"No," he said, in the same quiet, dull voice. "I want to go. I think you're devils. You've nearly killed me."

"I?" She laughed. "I didn't touch you."

"You're just as bad. You didn't stop her."

163

"Stop her? Why should I stop her? You agreed to take a thrashing, didn't you?"

"I want to go," he repeated stubbornly. "Just untie these chairs, please."

She narrowed her eyes again. She stooped and picked up the whip. She put it closely to his face. "You see this? You know the pain it can give you? Answer me."

He nodded his head.

"Well," she said, "I'm quite ready to give you another thrashing with it myself if I hear anything more about you wanting to go. Do you understand?"

He nodded again. He thought that he had better promise anything that she wanted. She would then untie the chairs, and he could grab his clothes and run. "All right," he said.

"All right, what?"

"All right, I won't say anything more about wanting to go."

She regarded him thoughtfully, put down the whip, and picked up the two stockings. "Put your wrists together."

He frowned at her. "What's the matter? Don't you trust me?"

"No. Put them together."

He sighed and obeyed. He watched his wrists being tied tightly. "I don't feel very much like it," he said. "It's been knocked out of me with that whip."

"It'll come back in a moment or two, and then you'll be as randy as a ram as a result of it." She tied an extra knot in the stockings. "There. You're safer now. You won't be able to run away, even if you do want to break your promise." She went to the door, which he had himself locked, and took the key out of its hole. She wondered where to put it. She saw that he was watching her. She went back to the centre of the

164

room, to the chairs over which he was lying, and passed on out of his line of vision. She quickly and silently opened a drawer and dropped the key in.

She walked back to him silently, lifting the hand-towel, now quite wet with his blood. She looked critically at his weals, saw that the bleeding had begun to stop, and went to the wash-basin. She wrung the blood out of the towel, turned on a tap to wash it all down the drain, and returned to him. She laid the towel over his buttocks again and patted it lightly to help the remaining blood to be absorbed. "I don't think you'll be able to go anywhere near the bed," she said. "We'd better do it on the floor." She knelt and began to untie the cords round the chair legs.

The red-head stirred on the bed. She gave a deep sigh of great satisfaction, raised her head and then, after a moment, her chest, turned over on her side, and slowly got off the bed. "Oho!" she said, looking at her victim and seeing the stocking tightly binding his wrists. "You're all helpless again. Are you waiting for another whipping?"

He looked up at her with a gaze of hatred. He opened his mouth to say something acid, saw the whip lying on the floor a few metres away from him, and closed his mouth again.

The blonde rose to her feet, the cords dangling in her hands. "You're free to get up now. Come on and to your stuff." She sat gracefully on the floor and lay backwards until she was stretched out. "It's a bit hard, but never mind. Better than having your blood all over the bed. Come on."

He rose stiffly from the chairs and stood erect. The bloody towel dropped to the floor.

The red-head loked at his penis. It was small and flaccid. She took it in her hands. "Is this my doing?"

165

she asked softly. "Did I make it go *so* small with my lovely whip?"

He looked at her again with hatred, but his penis began to stiffen. She was a very lovely girl.

"I don't think you like me very much," she said. "But never mind. I like *you*. I always have a great tenderness for anyone I've whipped."

"Come on, come on," said the blonde impatiently. "Don't just stand there. Get down here on top of me."

With his penis now fully erected again, and, indeed, feeling as randy as she had said he would, he knelt beside her and then lay down over her. She seized his penis and, opening her legs, guided it towards her hungry vagina. He gave a sigh of pleasure and abandoned himself to his reward.

The red-head picked up the dildo from the bed and quickly strapped it into position. She agitated it once or twice to make sure that the end that was inside her was comfortable. She knelt, and then lay over his back.

The blonde grunted with the extra weight upon her.

"Too heavy?" asked the red-head.

"No. It's all right," said the blonde. "Go ahead."

He turned his head in considerable surprise. "What's the game now?" He could not see the dildo that the red-head was wearing. He pulled irritably on the stockings that bound his wrists.

The blonde took a handful of his hair and pulled his head round again. "Nothing at all. Just get on with what you're going to do." She flexed her muscles and opened the mouth of her vagina. His penis slipped deliciously inside. "There," she said. "Isn't that nicer than talking all the time?"

"Yes," he said, and began to thrust and withdraw,

feeling his testicles enlarge with an unusually stimulated appetite.

The red-head raised her loins a little and put the
head of her dildo to his bottom.  She felt the
wetness of the remaining blood of his buttocks against
her own skin, and caught her breath with pleasure.
She guided the tip of the dildo to the mouth of his
anus.

As he felt the great thing enter his anus he gave
a cry and tried to turn his head again.  The blonde
caught his hair and prevented this.  "Lie still," she
hissed.  "Or I'll flog you to death!"

The red-head gave a thrust.  Her dildo slid
smoothly and deeply into his anus, and caused an
answering thrill of delight from the part inside her.

He felt the great instrument reaching far inside
him.

"She *is* a devil," he murmured, but found to his
surprise that she was giving him a good deal of
pleasure.  He sighed, found a more comfortable
position for his bound hands by putting them out
over the head of the girl upon whom he was lying,
and gave himself up to his rapturous thrusting and
withdrawing.

And as he thrust and withdrew with his penis, so
the red-head thrust and withdrew with her dildo.

### 7

An hour or so after lunch, Margarete Hansen
knocked at the door of Per Petersen's study.

"Ah," she said.  "Good.  You haven't gone back to
your office.  I was afraid I'd miss you."

"Do come in and sit down," he said.  "Did you
buy your things this morning?"

"I can't sit down now," she said. "I have to get back to the children." She stood just inside the door, looking at him with a smouldering expression.

"Did you buy the things?" he repeated, gazing at her with appreciation.

"Yes." She felt nervous, and was sure that she was showing it.

He looked at her enquiringly. "Is there anything the matter?"

She hesitated. "You said this morning something about the more the merrier."

"Yes?"

"When I asked you if you could stand being the victim of three sadistic women at the same time."

"Yes, yes," he said. "I remember very well."

"You said 'Why not? The more the merrier.'"

"Yes, I did. Why?"

She ran her tongue lightly over the under-part of her upper lip. "I've just had a telephone call from two friends of mine from Sweden."

"Yes?"

"One of them is a terrific sadist."

He opened his cigarette case and took out a cigarette. His pulse began to beat faster. "Go on." He smiled suddenly and waved his arm at a chair. "But why don't you come and sit down?" Things, he thought, were growing very interesting.

"I have to get back to the children," she repeated. She wondered whether she dared go on.

"What were you going to say then?"

"The other is a bit of a sadist from time to time but she's more of a nymphomaniac. And they're both terribly lovely. A red-head and a blonde."

His pulse gave a leap. He knew what she was going to say. "Go on," he repeated, in an encouraging tone of voice. His penis began to tingle.

168

She looked him full in the eyes. "Do you think you could stand five sadistic  women at the same time? Or rather, four and a nymphomaniac?  Would it still be a case of the more the merrier?"

This time it was his penis that leaped. "Yes," he said. "Definitely.  Why don't you ask them both for dinner with the rest of us?"

# PART SIX

## 1

Marlene Reitter and Erika Köstler were the first
to arrive. Per Petersen received them in his study.
He had wondered whether, since he was to have
five guests, he should receive them in the large salon.
This was a room, however, which had rarely been
used since his wife's death, and he preferred the
warmer atmosphere of his own domain. It was, in
fact, quite large enough for the entertainment of
five ladies.

Marlene was wearing a tightly-fitting dinner-dress
of tabac-coloured velvet, and, with her lovely ash-
blonde hair drawn back at the nape of her neck
in a chignon, again looked like a goddess from some
other world. In her eyes, as always when she visited
him in order to flog him, there was a burning light,
panther-like and menacing.

"Where is your children's governess?" she asked,

after she had introduced Erika Köstler. "I'm dying to meet her."

"She's upstairs with the children," he replied. "She'll be down in a minute."

He looked at Erika appreciatively. She was wearing a dark-red dress which he thought was made of a very swishy type of flimsy taffeta. She was, to his eyes, very lovely. He reflected that the evening was going to be extremely exciting. "And so you're a sadist, too?" he said conversationally as he offered a box of cigarettes first to Marlene and then to her.

"Very much of one," she answered.

He went close to her to light her cigarette. To his nostrils there came a smell — delightful, heavy, and heady — of sweetly perfumed rubber. He looked again at her dress and saw that it was made of rubberised crepe-de-chine, and not, after all, of taffeta. He glanced at her in some surprise. He had often heard of the fetish but he had not yet met anyone who possessed it. He felt, now, that it was not at all difficult to understand. She looked, and smelt, extremely fetching, and he longed for the time when he could press his body against her provocative dress, after he had taken off all his own clothes. His penis, which had erected the moment they came into the room, gave a tingling leap.

"What will you drink?" he asked, as calmly as he could. He addressed Marlene. He thought it might be unwise to show too clearly how attractive he found her assistant. "Sherry, perhaps?"

"That will be very nice," she said, crossing her lovely legs sensually and turning her burning expression on him.

"And you?" he asked Erika.

"Yes, please. The same."

172

He poured the drinks and brought them to the girls. "It's wonderful to see you again, Marlene. Did you have a good time in Paris?"

"Fairly good," she said. "But we were frustrated, of course."

"Why?" he asked. He knew perfectly well what she meant, for he had been told before of her masochistic English friend in Paris, but he wanted to hear the exciting words of her answer.

She smiled. She realised that he knew what she meant, but she gave him what he wanted. "My victim there can't be flogged as I want him to be flogged. He lives in an apartment with thin walls — not a house like this. It's very frustrating."

"But it's not frustrating here, eh?"

"Not *so* frustrating. But you have too many servants."

"There won't be any here after dinner."

She looked at him in surprise. "Oh? How have you arranged that?"

He laughed. "I didn't really arrange it. It just happened. It's the annual servants' ball tonight at the Town Hall. I've told them all that they can go."

She chuckled deliciously. "It seems that I chose my time rather well. Why didn't you tell me when I phoned you?"

"I must keep some surprises for you, my dear."

"You've already given me quite a big one."

"My children's governess?"

"Of course."

He drew deeply on his cigarette. "I have another one."

She smiled enquiringly. "Another governess?"

"No, another surprise. I don't know how you're going to take it."

"Try me."

He looked straight into her eyes. "You have two more assistants."

She raised her eyebrows. "*Two* more? You don't mean your governess *and* two more?"

"I do." He watched her expression closely but her eyes had a look now that he could not fathom.

"How did all this happen?" she asked, tapping the ash off the end of her cigarette on to the carpet. "Your house seems to be becoming a harem."

He realised that she was angry. "It's really nothing to do with me," he said in a conciliating tone of voice. "Miss Hansen, my governess, told me that two Swedish friends of hers have come to see her. I haven't met them yet."

"How does that make them my assistants?" Her voice was cold.

"They are sadists, too, it seems. At least, one of them is."

"So?" The coldness had turned into iciness.

He hesitated, and took a drink of his sherry to gain time. "So I told her to ask them for dinner."

"Go on. That's not all." She was looking at him now with her eyes half-closed. "Go on, dear Per."

He forced himself to meet her gaze. "For dinner and the — er — the party that follows."

She looked at him silently for a long moment. Then, unexpectedly, she laughed. "How absolutely delightful! Five women to flog you! My dear Per, I wonder whether you haven't signed your death warrant?"

He was only partly relieved by her laughter. "I thought it might amuse you," he said lamely.

Erika gave a chuckle from her chair. "And he's arranged for his servants to be out," she said to Marlene. "My God!"

He felt a sudden stab of fear. Perhaps he had been very unwise, after all. The thought of having five women to dinner, all of whom would give him a whipping after dinner, had excited him very much when he had first had it. Now that the whole thing was changing from a thought into a reality, however, he wondered whether he had not bitten off a great deal more than he would be able to chew. He turned his head to Erika and looked at her seriously. The way she had said "My God!" frightened him. The sight of her sitting in her slinky rubber dress, and the thought of taking her in his arms later, drove away his fear. This was the sort of evening that he had imagined in his masochistic day-dreams. It was happening at last. If he had to pay rather heavily for it later on — well, never mind; it was worth it. The exhilaration of the moment was worth anything at all that might happen later.

The study door opened. Margarete Hansen came into the room.

"Good evening," she said, looking rather at Per than at his guests. She had decided, as she came down the stairs, to conquer her feeling of jealousy. She had no right to it, she realised. Her manner, however, as she was introduced to Marlene and Erika, subtly suggested that she was not merely and simply a governess. Her appearance suggested nothing of the governess, either. She had dressed herself with extreme care, choosing a black dress that was aggressive in its stark simplicity. She wore but one piece of jewellery — a long and heavy chain of gold which she had looped round and round her neck and which fell, glintingly against the black, a little below her bosom. It was the only really expensive piece of jewellery that she possessed, but she was very satisfied with its effect.

Marlene regarded her with frank admiration. With her laughter of a few moments ago she had made a rapid decision. She would enjoy herself this evening, and would not spoil her enjoyment by giving way to stupid feelings of possessiveness for Per Petersen. He was free, after all, to live as he wanted. He owed no allegiance, no loyalty, no faithfulness, to her. It was infrequently, after all, that she came to Kiel to flog him. It would be unreasonable of her to expect him to regard her as his only tormentor. And if he was unwise enough to gather no fewer than five sadistic tormentors in his house on one and the same evening — well, that was his own business. He would certainly be made to suffer for it.

"You are very lovely, my dear," she said, and, to take away any possible hint of condescension, she looked at Per and added: "I don't think you will be taking any of those trips to London from now on."

His heart warmed as he realised that the ice was broken. He made no reply. He poured a glass of sherry for Margarete and listened gratefully to her spontaneous acceptance of Marlene's generous gesture. "I have heard only a little about you, Fraulein Reitter, but what I have heard has been — oh, *what* an understatement! You are — you are wonderful! No wonder he lives for your visits."

There was a knock on the study door. The butler entered. He looked at Per Petersen. "Excuse me, sir. Two friends of Miss Hansen have arrived."

"Show them in, please," said Per. He looked expectantly towards the door.

The blonde and the red-head came into the room. He caught his breath sharply at their beauty. He flashed a look at the three women who were already in the room and then looked back at the two newcomers. He reflected, with a feeling of considerable awe, that no other room over the length and breadth of Germany could contain such beautiful women as his did at this moment. And they were all gathered there for a very special sort of party — with him as the victim...

He was in a condition of considerable dither as he was introduced to the two friends of Margarete. He gathered that the blonde was called Birgitta and the red-head Anna. He did not catch their surnames, and he did not bother to ask for a repetition. Everyone would be on a Christian-name basis soon enough. "Do you speak German?" he asked, in as even a tone as he could. "We have two German ladies here who, I imagine, do not speak Swedish."

Margarete answered for her friends. "They speak German quite well."

Per introduced them to Marlene and Erika, mumbling over their surnames. Marlene was very gracious to them. She felt the gathering of another constraint, however, and felt it was up to her, more than anyone else, to dispel it at once. "How very nice to meet you," she said. "I understand we're members of the same club. The club of sadistic women, I mean."

Anna, the red-head, smiled at her warmly. "I am, myself. Birgitta, here, is a sort of honorary member."

"Nonsense," said Birgitta. "I can be just as much a member as you, when I'm given the chance. But you're such a greedy pig that I don't get the chance very often."

It was Margarete's heart that was warmed this time, as the ice was broken for the second time. She had worried a good deal about the advisability of introducing her two friends to the party, despite her employer's stated belief that the more would make the merrier.

A spontaneous chatter began among the five girls, and Per Petersen gave drinks to Birgitta and Anna, and refilled the other glasses.

"We're sorry we're not dressed for a dinner-party," Anna said to him. She and Birgitta were wearing their leather jackets with tightly-fitting skirts and high stiletto-heeled shoes. "We're on a hitch-hiking holiday."

"You look very nice indeed," said Per. "And very fetching, both of you."

"So do you," said Birgitta. "But I'm looking forward to seeing you without your clothes."

"That will be very soon," he said breathlessly. "Immediately after we've had dinner."

Marlene looked up at him. "How long to dinner?"

He glanced at the clock on his mantel. "About a quarter of an hour."

"Right." She stood up, reached for her bag, opened it, and took out two lengths of strong, fine cord. "Better lock the door for a moment. We don't want your butler marching in suddenly."

He nodded and went to the door to lock it.

The four girls stopped speaking and looked at her enquiringly.

She smiled at them. "This is something I always do when I have dinner with our host," she said. "It makes the dinner-table more interesting. There are always so many servants in the room that one has to watch one's conversation. But one doesn't have to watch all one's actions so much." She crooked a finger at Per. "Come here and open your trousers."

He walked up to her and undid the buttons of his flies.

She put her hand inside the trousers and brought out his enormously-erected penis and testicle-bag.

Birgitta caught her breath. Anna grinned at her,

and waggled a finger admonishingly. "This is most interesting," she said, looking at the cords which Marlene held in her other hand. "Whatever are you going to do?"

"Tie up his ball-bag," said Marlene, and made a loop in the end of one of her cords. "Then I can torture him whenever I feel bored at the dinner-table. I just pull on my end of the cord under the table."

"You have two cords tonight," said Per.

"That's for whoever sits on the other side of you," she said, and drew the loop tight around the testicle-bag, leaving the two testicles trapped between the bottom of their bag and the tightened cords. She made a loop in the other cord and fastened it in the same way around the testicle-bag. She gathered the other ends of the cords, a metre and a half long, into a sort of bow, and stuffed them inside his trousers. "Now you can button yourself up," she said. "And when we're at table you can unbutton yourself again, and bring everything out, and pass my own cord to me under the table as usual. Who has the other one is your own affair."

"You'll be on my right, of course," he said. "And I was thinking of putting Erika on my left."

"Erika will soon pick up the idea of the game, I've no doubt," said Marlene.

"Yes," said Erika. "I've picked it up already." She ran her hands over her dress just above her breasts. "I'm longing to pull on my own end."

"What a wonderful idea," breathed Margarete, watching Per button up his trousers. "I'm only sorry you haven't got three more lengths of cord."

"Do you dine with him as a rule?" asked Marlene.

"Yes," said Margarete. "Except when he has business dinners. Even then I sometimes do."

Marlene laughed. "It might be a little difficult

179

to put a cord on him for a business dinner. But you can do it whenever you're alone."

"And I certainly shall," said Margarete, with determination. "It's a wonderful idea."

With the cords around his testicle-bag making him walk a little stiffly, Per vent to the door and unlocked it. "Now that I'm decent again," he said, "it had better be unlocked. Dinner'll be announced in a minute or two."

"And I'm hungry," said Marlene.

"So am I," murmured Birgitta to Anna. "But not for food."

"Ssssh!" said Anna softly. "Behave yourself."

Birgitta pouted. "Behave yourself, you say! I wonder what they'd say if they could see that dildo in your bag."

"Ssssh, will you! They'll see it soon enough."

The door opened and the butler announced formally that dinner was served.

### 2

Per Petersen sat at the head of his table in a condition of even greater dither than he had been an hour before when he and his guests left the study. His penis had been stiffly erected for nearly two hours without interruption, and now seemed to have something like an ache at its base.

Marlene sat on his right and Erika on his left. At the beginning of the meal, when the backs of the butler and the maid were turned for an instant, he had unbuttoned his flies and taken out the cords. He had passed one cord under the table to the waiting hand of Marlene, and the other to Erika. He had then sat as closely as possible to the table, hiding his lap with the tablecloth. Marlene's first

180

pull on her cord had been gentle. Erika's, from lack of experience, had almost pulled his testicles off his body. He was glad that her subsequent pulls, throughout the length of the meal, had been less violent.

Birgitta sat on Erika's left, and Anna on Marlene's right. Excitedly, but enviously, they watched their host being tortured as he tried to eat naturally. They wished they could take part in the activities. Anna, however, was a little awed by the regality of Marlene and did not dare to ask for her end of the cord for a moment or two. Birgitta, on the other hand, had leaned to her right on one occasion and had felt under the table for Erika's cord. A warning cough from Erika had emphasised the danger of something being noticed by the servants, and she had at once let go of the cord, leaning on downwards to pretend to pick up a fallen napkin.

Margarete, at the other end of the table, opposite her employer, watched the effects of the pulling of the cords with a mixture of excitement and anxiety. It was exciting to her because a man's genital organs were being tortured under her eyes; it was worrying because she felt that one or other of the servants could not fail to notice that their employer was not sitting in his usual relaxed posture but was from time to time making jerky movements on the seat of his chair.

At last, the dessert was served, and the servants left the room.

"So," said Marlene to him, giving a pull on her cord, "we are six tonight. You, my dear, and five women who are now going to flog you a good deal. The question is, where shall we do it?"

"There's no need to worry about noise," said Margarete. "The servants will all be out. And the children are far away at the other end of the house."

181

"Exactly," said Marlene. "I usually flog him in his bedroom — because it's the safest place from the noise point of view. But it's not necessary tonight, and five of us may be rather on top of one another. So where?"

Margarete looked at Per. "May I suggest the main salon? There's plenty of room — and there are plenty of sofas and things."

"I approve of that," said Birgitta. "I mean the sofas."

"I've been wondering," said Per, "which of you two is the sadist and which the nymph. You're the nymph, aren't you?"

"Yes," said Birgitta, simply. "But I can be quite a sadist too. I am feeling one tonight, in fact."

"*Now* who is the pig?" said Anna.

Per raised his eyes at her enquiringly.

"You'll soon see what she means," said Birgitta. "She has another perversion, on top of her sadism — and I tell her she's a greedy pig most of the time. You'll soon see what it is."

Per laughed. "All right, I'll be patient." He turned to Erika, the warmth of whose body was causing her rubberised dress to give off a very heady and exciting perfume. "And you, too — you have another perversion, haven't you?"

She blushed slightly. "This dress?"

"Yes."

"Yes, I love anything made of rubber."

He nodded his head. "Looking at you, I think I'm beginning to like it too."

Marlene said : "So, what do you say to using your big salon?"

He turned to her. "Very well. It's probably the best place." He was slightly disinclined, now that the moment had arrived, to leave the safety of the dining-room. He glanced round his table again at the five lovely girls who were going to thrash him, and his masochism overcame his fear. He said: "Let's move there, then — if you're ready."

"Have you still got that ladder?" asked Marlene.

"Yes," he said.

"Go and get it. And bring it to the salon. We'll be there waiting for you."

"A ladder?" said Margarete. "What for?"

Marlene smiled at her. "A ladder is a wonderful thing to tie a man to if you want to flog him and play with him a little, too."

## 3

The scene in the main salon half an hour later would have delighted the hearts of both the Marquis de Sade and the Baron Sacher-Masoch.

Per Petersen, stripped of all his clothes, was standing on the bottom rung of a three-metre-high ladder that leant against one of the walls. His legs were slightly open because his ankles were tightly bound to the sides of the ladder. His arms were stretched above his head, with his wrists tied, too, to the sides of the ladder. His testicles, still bound with the two lengths of cord, and his erected penis lay in the empty space between two of the rungs. He was silent because he had been gagged with Anna's panties.

On a piano-stool on the other side of the ladder sat Margarete. She held the ends of the two cords in her hands and pulled on them lightly but firmly as she put his penis in and out of her mouth. From time to time she lifted her hands up to his breast, and scratched and squeezed his nipples with her long pointed fingernails. On the floor by her side were the instruments that she had bought that

183

morning — a long whalebone riding-switch, a cruel-looking dogwhip, and a heavy leather razor-strop. She had not yet used any of them but she knew that a long evening was in front of them all and she was content to wait her turn. She had stripped herself down to her brassiere and panties.

It was Marlene now who was using one of her whips, a savage instrument made of two strips of leather with square edges. She had taken off all her clothes and put on her long black rubber cloak to protect her flesh from the blood which she knew would soon begin to fly. For the moment, she was whipping only his buttocks, as she usually did on her visits to him. She knew that he was not so much of a masochist as to take willingly a whipping across his back, but she also knew that such gentleness could not, in these circumstances, last for very long. With no fewer than four other girls ready and waiting to take her place, somebody was sure to become over-excited and start on his back. The thought occurred to her that when that happened it would be nobody's fault but his own. If he was so unwise as to fill his house with no fewer than five bloodthirsty women at the same time, he had it coming to him...

She altered her aim and began to lash him across his shoulders. His body flexed and jerked as though he was receiving terrible electric shocks. No sound but a low, continuous, strangled moan came from him. Anna'a panties had been thrust too far into his mouth.

Anna herself stood a little way away to the left of the ladder. She was wearing nothing but her great dildo and her whip looped around her neck. She watched the thrashing with half-closed eyes and heaving breasts, feeling the tide of insane rapture ebb and flow over her senses.

To the right of the ladder stood Erika. She had taken off all her clothes too, but she had put her flimsy rubberised-silk dress back over her naked body. She had opened its bodice and pulled out her breasts. As she watched the thrashing she was playing with her nipples with her fingertips.

Birgitta, the nymphomaniac, was in a pitiful condition. She lay, quite naked, on her stomach on one of the sofas nearby, listening to — but trying not to watch — this first thrashing. As each lash swished through the air and cut into flesh with its *zmak* of pseudo-finality she gave a convulsive quiver. She felt as though a feather had lightly touched the lips of her vagina, maddening her with desire. She wondered desperately how long it would be before she could take this man and put him down beside her. She wanted to cry out to Anna to come and rape her with her great dildo, but she knew that Anna was waiting only to be given a turn with her whip and would not even hear her.

Marlene felt herself tiring. She felt slightly surprised because she knew that she had delivered only about forty lashes, and she could usually deliver up to a hundred before needing a rest. She reflected that she must be rather tired from the journey. She would give way to someone else, and sit and watch the rest. There was a good deal more to come. It would be exciting to watch it, and to see how much Per Petersen could take before he fainted.

She let her whip fall to her side. She looked round the ladder at Margarete. "Would you like to take over now?"

Margarete took her mouth away from his penis. In spite of the terrible pain he was receiving it was still erected, but he knew that it would go quickly soft unless someone else took her place at once. He wondered whether anyone would.

He did not wonder for long. As Margarete stood up from the piano-stool and picked up her instruments, Birgitta jumped off the sofa and ran to the stool. "I'll do this for a little," she said breathlessly. She opened her mouth and engulfed the saliva-wetted penis. She took the cords and tugged on them sharply.

Anna laughed. "Patience running thin, eh?" She took hold of her own false penis and agitated it roughly, so that she should be tantalised by the part that lay inside her vagina. She realised that her own patience was running thin, too. She did not know which she wanted more at that moment — to whip, or to push her dildo into someone. She knew only that she would have to wait some time before she could do anything at all to her host. She looked at Erika, standing on the other side of the ladder in her provocative red dress, and wondered whether she had been right or wrong when, at the dinner table, she had sensed some indefinable suggestion of lesbianism about the girl. It would be pleasant to use the dildo on her... She moved her position casually, and sauntered up beside her.

Margarete studied her newly-bought instruments. "I'm not hurrying," she said to the company in general, "because I expect he needs a moment or two to get his breath back." She was in a quandary. She wanted to use all three instruments, one after the other — but she knew that, out of politeness to the guests, she would have to content herself with only one. They were obviously impatient to take their turn. Which, then, should she use? The lovely slim switch? The whip? The razor-strop? A whip had already been used, and the red-head called Anna was wearing hers like a necklace around her neck. She was clearly going to take it off and use it when her turn came. That would be at least two whips used. Perhaps she herself should offer a little variety.

She made up her mind, put the whip and the strop on a chair, and took the switch into her whipping hand.

Anna looked at Erika with open admiration. "You look absolutely eatable," she said, and tentatively put out a hand to the breasts which lay exposed in her opened bodice. Erika's reaction would show whether she had any lesbianism.

Erika did not move away from her touch. She let Anna's hand play over her nipples. Her shoulders went back perceptibly as she strained her muscles to take the full lascivious pleasure. After a moment she put her hand on Anna's dildo and agitated it lightly.

"Be rougher," said Anna. "Then I can feel it better inside me."

Margarete went to the side of the ladder. "It's going to be me this time," she said. "And I'm going to use my new switch on your bottom and legs. I'll use my other things another day. Would you like to know how many lashes I'm going to give you now with the switch?"

He nodded his head. His eyes were distraught with fear. He wished he had not allowed himself to be gagged. He could then have had some chance of calling this whole terrible thing off. Not much, certainly — but he would have had more than he had now, gagged as he was with these sweet-smelling panties. He wished he had never thought of the party at all. One woman in his house to whip him was quite enough. Five was madness. They would flog him into insensibility. They might even kill him. And yet his penis remained stiff and hungry as it slid in and out of the mouth of the blonde Birgitta. Despite the agony he had suffered, he was still receiving a certain amount of pleasure.

"Fifty," said Margarete. "A nice round number, don't you think?" She went back to her whipping position and lifted her switch. It slashed down and cut into the flesh of his legs. His body jerked again as though it had received another electric shock.

"This will go on for some time," said Anna. "Why don't we amuse ourselves on a sofa while it's going on?"

"That's not a bad idea," said Erika, looking down at the dildo. "You mean with this, of course."

"Yes," said Anna, putting her other hand now to the naked breasts. "And something else, if you could take it. I'd love to do it."

Erika raised her eyes to the whip round Anna's neck. "That?"

"Yes, I'd love to whip you a little."

Erika shook her head. "Not with that." She was quite prepared to accept a beating — the idea, in fact excited her greatly — but she would not allow this terrible whip to be used. Only her adored Marlene could use a whip on her.

"I'd be quite gentle," said Anna.

Erika shook her head again. She nodded in the direction of Margarete's razor-strop lying on a nearby chair. "But you can use that if you like."

Anna looked at the strop. It would give more pain that Erika imagined. "I'd like to," she said. "It would be delicious. Then I could put you over my knees and make your bottom red-hot." She waited for Margarete to aim and deliver another slash, and said: "May I borrow your razor-strop for a few minutes?"

"Certainly," said Margarete, without looking

round. She aimed again and slashed. "Nine," she murmured. "Forty-one to come." She saw that blood was beginning to spatter over the floor near her feet. She kicked a nearby rug a little further away. It would be easy to wipe the blood away from the polished parquet — it might be a wonderful idea to make Per do it himself, on his hands and knees, with everything flogging him while he did it — but a certain care had to be taken of the rugs and furniture. When she finished her whipping with this switch she would spread the car-cover over one of the sofas. He would never be able to lie down otherwise. She slashed again. "Ten," she said. "Forty to come." She felt light-headed with sadistic ecstasy. Life had never been so wonderful. This man was so utterly in her power. She could whip him to within a second or two of his life, if she wanted to. She began to feel that she wanted to, very much indeed. "Eleven," she almost crooned. "Thirty-nine to come."

Anna had taken the strop and sat on one of the sofas. She opened her legs to make a wide lap for Erika to lie on. Her great dildo stood frighteningly up into the air. She patted one of her knees. "Come on. Lie down."

Erika lifted the skirt of her flimsy dress and lay down over her lap.

"Wait a minute," said Anna. "Let's put this into you first. Open your legs. Lie a little over on your side." She guided the head of the dildo to Erika's wet vagina, opened its lips with her fingers, and slowly inserted the instrument. It slid easily up Erika's passage, making her catch her breath with delight. "Now lie flat," said Anna. Erika obeyed, and felt the dildo slide further up and into her. She put her forward in front of her and took hold of a cushion. She hugged it tightly to her breasts.

Anna took the heavy leather strop in her right hand, and lifted the skirt completely away from the delicate buttocks. "Oh," she said, as she saw the weals of Marlene's whipping of the day before, "somebody else has been doing this to you recently. Man or woman?"

"Woman," said Erika.

"It must have been quite a whipping. Let me see whether I can give you a better one." She raised the strop and struck hard at the buttocks. They gave a quiver as though the muscles beneath them were trying to escape. Erika felt the dildo thrust more deeply into her. Anna's own end of the instrument gave its answering stab of rapture. She began to strike hard and rhythmically.

Behind the ladder, Birgitta stood up suddenly. She pressed herself closely against the wood and put the dripping penis between her legs. She opened her vagina lips and forced its head into her passage. Because of the angle at which the ladder was leaning against the wall, she found great difficulty in staying in this position. Quickly she took the cords which dangled from his testicle-bag, separated them, and tied them tightly round her hips. This enabled her to keep his penis inside her, without using too much of her own strength. She put up her hands and took hold of a rung above her head. Supporting her angled weight like this, she began to thrust and withdraw her genitals over the penis that she had engulfed.

Marlene sat in her long black cloak with her legs crossed and with a half-smile playing on her lips. She saw that Erika and Anna were reaching a state of frenzy with what they were doing to each other. She was a little piqued at Erika's having gone so willingly to the sofa with Anna, but she gave a mental shrug and determined to deliver a severe

190

punishment to the girl when she got her alone. For the moment she would not interfere. She turned her eyes to the ladder. Birgitta, it seemed, was having a very good time herself. Her eyes were closed, her lips open, her teeth showing. She was moaning with utter and final abandon. Per Petersen was also moaning, of course, from the agony of Margarete's switch, but it seemed that he was answering some of the thrusts of Birgitta, and so, perhaps, was not in such a dire condition as she would have imagined.

It would have been a gross exaggeration to say that Per was enjoying himself. The agony in his bottom and legs was enough, he thought, to drive him insane, but, nevertheless, he had received a good deal of pleasure from the mouth of Birgitta and now he was receiving even more from her vagina, even though her weight pulling on the cords round his testicles gave him spams of unendurable pain. Inexorably, however, his juices gathered. When Margarete's switch cut into the fleshy part of his legs, they were driven away momentarily, but when her switch cut into his buttocks he received a stimulation that brought them back in a rush. He knew that, if he was lucky, he would have a culmination within a few moments.

Birgitta sensed this, and began to put a little control on her thrusts. She wanted her own fulfilment to be timed to his — if his own had any chance of coming. "Could you please," she gasped to Margarete, "concentrate on his bottom for a little while? I think he may be coming and it will stop him if the pain is too terrible."

"Certainly," said Margarete. "I'm all in favour of his having some fun too, if he can." She lashed at the buttocks. "Thirty-four. Sixteen to come. But what makes you think the pain there is any less terrible?"

"I don't know why it is," panted Birgitta, "but it usually seems to be more bearable."

"Is that so?" Margarete put more strength into her lash. "Thirty-five. Fifteen to come."

Ten lashes later, Per Petersen's body seemed to melt in a white-hot furnace of searing, agonising — yet blissful — rapture. Birgitta's body went as tense as a tightened spring as the sensation for which she craved poured over her nerves.

Margarete realised what was happening, and gave the last five lashes at the same speed but very hard. When she at last let her blood-dripping switch fall to her side, she was astonished to see that her victim was still ejaculating himself into Brigitta. "Good heavens!" she murmured, dropping into a chair. "What a man!"

Marlene took a cigarette from a box on the table beside her. She lit it and said: "I suppose we'd better have a bit of an interval now, hadn't we? And something to drink. You've probably had quite enough of whipping for the time being. Birgitta, I think, won't be very interested now." She turned her head and looked at the frenzied activities of Erika and Anna on the sofa. "And those two are too busy, far too busy."

"And yourself?" said Margarete. "Don't you want to have another go?"

"Not yet," said Marlene. "Later, of course. But I think I'll untie him for a little while. He'll need a rest." She rose to her feet and helped Birgitta untie the cords around her hips. Then she began to undo the bonds of the bleeding man.

Dully, he realised that his body had been drained of sexual feeling. He felt as though he was on fire, burning excruciatingly. The pain was terrible, shocking in its intensity. He began to feel a smouldering anger.

He lay quite still, in his agony, until all his bonds were loose. He continued to lie still while his gag was removed. Then slowly, stiffly, he stepped down from the bottom on which he had been standing. He turned round.

"Oh damn," said Margarete, totally relaxed in her chair. "I forgot to put car-cover over a sofa for you."

"I'll do it," said Marlene. She went to where it was lying, and brought it to one of the sofas. "Come on, Per. You'll be glad to lie down for a bit, I suppose." She threw the cover open and spread it, rubber side upwards, over the sofa.

While she was doing this, Per stooped painfully and picked up the whip which she had used on him. Then he moved quickly to the whip which Margarete had bought during the morning. His anger had turned into a wild, berserk desire for revenge. He put Margarete's whip into his other hand. He moved quickly up behing Marlene, snatched her long cloak away from her naked body, and slashed her, with her own cutting two-thonged whip, across her back. She screamed and turned. Another slash caught her full across her breasts. A back-hand swipe with Margarete's whip cut into the soft flesh of her stomach. She screamed wildy and threw herself on to the sofa, trying desperately to protect herself with the folds of the car-cover.

With a blazing light in his eyes, Per advanced to the sofa from which Anna and Erika were now gazing at him, speechlessly, with terror in their eyes. It seemed as though the power of movement had left them, they sat so still. Per was on them in a second, lashing and slashing with both his whips. At this, they came to life and began to scream. It was difficult for either of them to move out of the way of the lashes because Anna's great dildo was deep inside Erika.

Per lashed with all his might, hitting blindly, not caring where he struck. Anna lay back on the sofa, grabbing cushions with which to protect her face and breasts.

Birgitta, still, standing behind the ladder, looked on and felt she should do something... *something*. But it was quite out of the question to go anywhere near those flailing whips. There must be something else she could do...

The same thought was running through Margarete's head. *What* could she do? She had not the courage ot go and try to take hold of his arms. In any case she would not have sufficient strength.

She saw Marlene's long and voluminous cloak lying on the floor. Yes, with that she might do something. She could throw it over his head perhaps, and then they might be able to overpower him. But she would have to be quick, while he was still whipping Anna and Erika... She could move up behind him...

She moved quickly, picked up the heavy rubber cloak, nudged Marlene to show what was her intention. She ran up quickly behind him, waited for her moment, and threw the cloak over his head.

He gave a roar of anger and tried to throw it away, but her arms were round his waist now, her hands locked. "Come on, quickly!" she screamed. "Come on, help me! Marlene, Birgitta, Anna, Erika — all of you! Come on!" She clung to him as he furiously tried to throw her off, his movements hampered by the cloak over his head and shoulders.

Birgitta came suddenly to life. She raced across the room and flung herself to the floor, her arms around his legs.

Marlene got up quickly, disengaged herself from the folds of the car-cover, and ran to Margarete's aid. She gave him a great push. He crashed over on to the floor.

By the time Anna and Erika had disengaged themselves from the dildo, it was nearly over. Per struggled on for a moment or two and then felt his remaining strength ebb and die away. He let himself go limp. There was now no anger left in his body. There was only a dreadful fear.

"Bring some ropes," he heard Marlene say.

He felt his ankles and them his wrists being securely bound. When he was quite helpless again the cloak was pulled away from his head. He gazed up at the five girls. He was shocked to see the weals on the breasts and stomachs of three of them. He was even more shocked to see the expression on their faces.

"What have you done?" asked Marlene, very quietly. "What *have* you done?"

He made no reply.

"You really *have* signed something like your death warrant now," she said.

"We may not actually kill you, of course — but I doubt whether you'll be able to walk for the next few months." She leaned forward to where her whip was lying. She looked round at the other girls. "Let's do this quite deliberately," she said. "Let's each get a whip and flog him here on the floor. Let's flog him, I mean, all together — all at once."

Without a word the girls provided themselves with whips and stood in a circle round him.

He opened his mouth to speak, and then closed it again. It would be useless to plead for mercy.

"Are we all ready?" said Marlene.

"Wait a second," said Margarete. "We'd better gag him again."

"I'd like to hear him scream," said Anna.

"The children," said Margarete. "I know they're at the other end of the house, but —"

Anna's panties were thrust and fastened into his mouth again.

"Ready now?" said Marlene. "Quite ready?"

They nodded their heads, and poised their whips.

A very terrible sound began to fill the room...

## THE END

# DELECTUS BOOKS

'The world's premiere publisher of classic erotica.' *Bizarre.*

## THE MISTRESS & THE SLAVE

A Parisian gentleman of position & wealth begins a romantic liaison with a poor but voluptuous young woman and falls wholly under her spell. The perversity of her nature, with its absolute domination over him, eventually culminates in a tragic ending.

'But, my child, you don't seem to understand what a Mistress is. For instance: your child your favourite daughter, might be dying and I should send you to the Bastille to get me a twopenny trinket. You would go, you would obey! Do you understand?' - 'Yes!' he murmured, so pale and troubled that he could scarcely breathe. 'And you will do everything I wish?' - 'Everything, darling Mistress! Everything! I swear it to you!'

Delectus 1995 hbk 160p. £19.95

## THE PETTICOAT DOMINANT OR, WOMAN'S REVENGE

An insolent aristocratic youth, Charles, makes an unwelcome, though not initially discouraged pass at his voluptuous tutoress Laura. In disgust at this transgression she sends Charles to stay with her cousin Diane d'Erebe, in a large country house inhabited by a coterie of governesses. They put him through a strict regime of corrective training, involving urolagnia, and enforced feminisation dressing him in corsets and petticoats to rectify his unruly character. Written under a pseudonym by London lawyer Stanislas de Rhodes, and first published in 1898 by Leonard Smithers' 'Erotica Biblion Society', Delectus have reset the original into a new edition.

'Frantic...breathless...spicy...restating the publisher's place at the top of the erotic heap.' *Divinity.* 'A great classic of fetish erotica...A marvellous period piece.' *Bizarre.*

Delectus 1994 hbk 120p. £19.95

# A GUIDE TO THE CORRECTION OF YOUNG GENTLEMEN
*By A Lady*

The ultimate guide to Victorian domestic discipline, lost since all previously known copies were destroyed by court order nearly seventy years ago.

'Her careful arrangement of subordinate clauses is truly masterful.' *The Daily Telegraph*. 'I rate this book as near biblical in stature' *The Naughty Victorian*. 'The lady guides us through the corporal stages with uncommon relish and an experienced eye to detail...An absolute gem of a book.' *Zeitgeist*. 'An exhaustive guide to female domination.' *Divinity*. 'Essential reading for the modern enthusiast with taste.' *Skin Two*.

Delectus 1994 hbk with a superb cover by Sardax 140p with over 30 illustrations. £19.95

## FRÉDÉRIQUE: THE TRUE STORY OF A YOUTH TRANSFORMED INTO A GIRL
*Don Brennus Alera*

A young orphan is left in the charge of his widowed aristocratic aunt, Baroness Saint-Genest. This elegant and wealthy lady teaches Frédérique poise & manners and, with eager help from her maid, Rose, transforms him into a young woman, while at the same time keeping him as her personal slave and sissy maid, using discipline to ensure complete obedience. Originally published by The Select Bibliotheque, Paris in 1921, this marvellous transvestite tale has been translated into florid English for the first time by Valerie Orpen. The story of Frederique's subjugation and feminisation is accompanied by 16 charming and unique illustrations, reproduced from the original French edition.

Delectus 1995 hbk 160p. £19.95

## FRIDA: THE TRUE STORY OF A YOUNG MAN BECOMING A YOUNG WOMAN
*Don Brennus Alera*

The stunning sequel to Frederique follows our hero to a new Mistress and new experiences. Translated by Valerie Orpen. (Call for publication details...)

## WHITE STAINS - ANAIS NIN & FRIENDS

Lost classic of 1940s erotica first published by Samuel Roth in New York. This collection of six sensual yet explicit short stories closely resemble the literary style of Nin's known erotic works, *Little Birds* and *Delta of Venus* and is thought to have been written for an Oklahoma oil millionaire, Roy M. Johnson, who is said to have paid a dollar per page. This facsimile reproduction of the original also contains an explicit sex manual, *'Love's Cyclopaedia'*, originally published with the stories, and an introduction by C.J. Scheiner examining all the evidence for the Anais Nin attribution. Renowned Paris photographer, Irina Ionesco, provides a stunning cover to this remarkable book.

Delectus 1995 hbk 220p. £19.95

## THE ROMANCE OF CHASTISEMENT; OR, REVELATIONS OF SCHOOL AND BEDROOM
### By An Expert

*The Romance* is filled with saucy tales comprising headmistresses taking a birch to the bare backsides of schoolgirls, women whipping each other, men spanking women, an aunt whipping her nephew and further painful pleasures.

Delectus have produced a complete facsimile of the rare 1888 edition of this renowned and elegant collection of verse, prose and anecdotes on the subject of the Victorian English gentleman's favourite vice: Flagellation!

'One of the all time flagellation classics.' *The Literary Review*, 'In an entirely different class...A chronicle of punishment, pain and pleasure.' *Time Out*. 'A classic of Victorian vice.' *Forum*, 'A very intense volume...a potent, single-minded ode to flagellation.' *Divinity*, 'A delightful book of awesome contemporary significance...the book is beautifully written.' *Daily Telegraph*. 'Stylishly reproduced and lovingly illuminated with elegant graphics and pictures...written in a style which is charming, archaic and packed with fine detail.' *The Redeemer.*

Delectus 1993 hbk 160p. £19.95

## PAINFUL PLEASURES

A fascinating miscellany of relentless spankomania comprising letters, short stories. Originally published in New York 1931, Delectus have produced a complete facsimile complemented by ten beautiful line illustrations vividly depicting punishment scenes from the book.

Both genders end up with smarting backsides in such stories as *'The Adventures of Miss Flossie Evans,'* and, probably the best spanking story ever written, *'Discipline at Parame'* in which a stern and uncompromising disciplinarian brings her two cousins Elsie and Peter to meek and prompt obedience. An earlier section contains eight genuine letters and an essay discussing the various merits of discipline and corporal punishment.

The writing is of the highest quality putting many of the current mass market publishers to shame, and Delectus into a class of its own.

'An extraordinary collection...as fresh and appealing now as in its days of shady celebrity...especially brilliant...another masterpiece...a collectors treasure.' *Paddles.* 'An American S&M classic'. *The Bookseller,* 'Sophisticated...handsomely printed... classy illustrations...beautifully bound.' *Desire.* 'For anyone who delights in the roguish elegance of Victorian erotica...this book is highly recommended.' *Lust Magazine.* 'A cracking good read.' *Mayfair.*

Delectus 1995 hbk in imperial purple d/j 272p. £19.95.

## MEMOIRS OF A DOMINATRICE
*Jean Claqueret & Liane Laure*

An elegant and aristocratic Governess recalls her life and the experiences with the young men in her charge. Translated from the French by Clair Auclair from the French edition first published The Collection des Orties Blanches, in Paris, during the 1920s. Illustrated with reproductions of the 10 Jim Black drawings from the original French edition.

Delectus 1995 hbk 140p. £19.95

## MODERN SLAVES
*Claire Willows*

From the same publishers as *Painful Pleasures* and *The Strap Returns*, this superb novel, from 1931, relates the story of young Laura who is sent from New York to stay with her uncle in England. However, through a supposed case of mistaken identity, she finds herself handed over to a mysterious woman, who had engineered the situation to suit her own ends. She is whisked away to an all female house of correction, Mrs. Wharton's Training School, in darkest Thurso in the far north of Scotland. Here she undergoes a strict daily regime under the stern tutelage of various strict disciplinarians, before being sold to Lady Manville as a maid and slave. There she joins two other girls and a page boy, William, all of whom Lady Manville disciplines with a unique and whole hearted fervour.

Delectus have produced a beautiful facsimile reproduction of the original Gargoyle edition from the golden decade of American erotica, including 10 superb art-deco style line drawings explicitly depicting scenes from the novel.

Delectus 1995 hbk in imperial purple d/j 288p. £19.95


## THE STRAP RETURNS: NEW NOTES ON FLAGELLATION
A superb and attractive facsimile reproduction of an anthology from 1933, originally issued in New York by the same publishers of two other Delectus titles, *Painful Pleasures* and *Modern Slaves*.

This remarkable book contains letters, authentic episodes and short stories including '*A Governess Lectures on the Art of Spanking*', '*A Woman's Revenge*' & '*The Price of a Silk Handkerchief or, How a Guilty Valet was Rewarded*', along with decorations and six full page line drawings by Vladimir Alexandre Karenin.

Delectus 1995 hbk 220p. £19.95

## MASOCHISM IN AMERICA OR, MEMOIRS OF A VICTIM OF FEMINISM
*Pierre Mac Orlan*

A French erotic classic, first published in the 1920s, by surrealist, war hero, and renowned popular thriller writer, Pierre Mac Orlan, this crafted collection of erotic vignettes provides a male masochistic odyssey through America.

Translated, for the first time into English by Alexis Lykiard, and including the five J. Sonrel illustrations from the French original.

Delectus 1995 hbk 200p. £19.95

## WHITE WOMEN SLAVES
*Don Brennus Alera*

Set in America's deep south in the years just preceding the American Civil War this book follows the life of Englishman, Lord Ascot, and his associates in the State of Louisiana. Originally published by The Select Bibliotheque in 1910 and written by the prolific author of another Delectus title, *Frédérique*, this book contains all eight original illustrations.

Delectus 1996 hbk 270p. £19.95

## PAGEANT OF LUST
*Peter Linden*

Another classic of American erotica from the 1940s in which the erotic encounters are so frequent and so relentless that the book has an almost delirious quality that only sensual abandonment can bring. The book is produced in facsimile along with the eight Francis Bacon style plates by Raymond Milne and an introduction by C.J. Scheiner.

Delectus 1996 hbk 200p. £19.95

## THE SEDUCING CARDINAL'S AMOURS, THE VOLUPTUOUS NIGHT & THE AMATORY ADVENTURES OF TILLY TOUCHITT

Three erotic classics bound in one volume, originally published by Edward Avery, one of the most active of the late Victorian erotic publishers. The first concerns the conquests of a debauched Jesuit Cardinal as he seduces his way across Northern Italy in the Renaissance and is illustrated with six explicit and rare engravings by Frederillo.

The real author of *The Voluptuous Night* is thought to be Baron Denon (1747-1825), a Belgian aristocrat of whom little is known. The story revolves around the a gentleman who spends a night of passion with his lovers best friend, Madame Terville, and her maid in a luxurious Chateau. The writing is highly stylised, the language flowery & decadent, the imagery luscious and dreamlike, and at the end of the night the man himself is still not sure whether the night's affairs had all been a dream. Dark secret passages, a room of mirrors, temples to Priapus, exquisite gardens and pavilions are just some the features that make this a most extraordinary novella.

The third book comprises a long letter of confession from a young woman who could not wait until marriage to loose her maidenhead!

Delectus 1996 hbk 180p. £19.95

## COMING SOON IN HARDBACK:

Happy Tears, Gynecocracy, A Nocturnal Meeting, Lustful Lucy, With Rod & Bum, The Amorous Widow, Maidenhead Stories, & many more.

# DELECTUS PAPERBACKS

## 120 DAYS OF SODOM - ADAPTED FOR THE STAGE BY NICK HEDGES FROM THE NOVEL BY THE MARQUIS DE SADE

Four libertines take a group of young adults and four old whores to a deserted castle, there they engage in a four month marathon of cruelty, debasement, and debauchery. The award winning play now available from Delectus, featuring stills from the London production and a revealing interview with the director.

'A bizarre pantomime of depravity that makes the Kama Sutra read like a guide to personal hygiene.' *What's On*. 'If you missed the play, you definitely need to get the book.' *Rouge*. 'Unforgettable...their most talked about publication so far.' *Risque*.

Delectus 1991 pbk 112p. £6.95

## SCREAM, MY DARLING SCREAM!
*ANGELA PEARSON*

Collection of six female domination stories from the author of the book you are now reading.

Delectus 1996 pbk 200p. £9.99

## COMING SOON IN PAPERBACK:

The Whipping Club, The Libertine, Whipsdom, Lover, The Whipping Post, Satan in Paris and many more.

---

## COMING SOON:

DELECTUS VAMPIRE CLASSICS. A new series featuring some of the best Vampire tales ever written, many appearing for the first time in English.